Christmas Eve Nightmare

Ashleigh noticed a rustling in the clean straw bedding on the floor. Suddenly a tiny brown mouse darted out and scampered across the horse's stall. The horse snorted and pulled hard on his halter, but Ashleigh held him firmly.

Then everything seemed to happen at once. One of the stable cats shot through the open stall door to leap on the mouse, which quickly dove into the thick straw. With a whinny of fear, the high-strung racer ripped his halter out of Ashleigh's hand and lunged out of the stall, nearly running Samantha down.

Ashleigh rushed after him. Scared now, and panicking in his fear, the horse kicked out with his back hooves and caught Ashleigh squarely in the side with a powerful thrust. She fell backward, and a shock of pain exploded through her body. With a low groan, she collapsed on the floor and rolled up into a ball, clutching her pregnant belly.

Collect all the books in the THOROUGHBRED series:

#1   A Horse Called Wonder
#2   Wonder's Promise
#3   Wonder's First Race
#4   Wonder's Victory
#5   Ashleigh's Dream
#6   Wonder's Yearling
#7   Samantha's Pride
#8   Sierra's Steeplechase
#9   Pride's Challenge
#10   Pride's Last Race
#11   Wonder's Sister
#12   Shining's Orphan
#13   Cindy's Runaway Colt
#14   Cindy's Glory
#15   Glory's Triumph

Throughbred Super Editions:

Ashleigh's Christmas Miracle
Ashleigh's Diary

Also by Joanna Campbell:

Battlecry Forever!
Star of Shadowbrook Farm

THOROUGHBRED

Ashleigh's Christmas Miracle

JOANNA CAMPBELL

HarperPaperbacks
A Division of HarperCollins*Publishers*

HarperPaperbacks   *A Division of* HarperCollins*Publishers*
10 East 53rd Street, New York, N.Y. 10022

Produced by Daniel Weiss Associates, Inc., 33 West 17th Street, New York, New York 10011.

First printing: December 1994

Printed in the United States of America

HarperPaperbacks and colophon are trademarks of HarperCollins*Publishers*

10 9 8 7 6 5 4

"MERRY CHRISTMAS, WONDER." ASHLEIGH GRIFFEN dropped a kiss on the velvety nose of the retired champion Thoroughbred racer, then wrapped her arms around the mare's neck and gave her a hug.

"You two have had a lot of Christmas Eves together," said Mike Reese, Ashleigh's husband.

Ashleigh smiled. "You're not kidding. This is our twelfth one. I can hardly believe it."

Ashleigh glanced around at all of her beloved horses in the nearby stalls of the mares' barn at Whitebrook Farm, the training and breeding farm that Ashleigh, Mike, and Mike's father, Gene Reese, owned outside of Lexington, Kentucky. When Ashleigh was a little girl, she and her parents had started the tradition of giving all the horses special treats on Christmas Eve. It was one of her favorite holiday customs.

Taking a carrot out of the bag she was carrying, she fed it to the elegant mare, who delicately lipped it up.

"Hi! Thought we'd find you out here." Ashleigh and Mike turned around when they heard the cheerful voice of Samantha McLean. Ashleigh smiled at Samantha, who was one of her best friends. She, her father, and her stepmother, Beth, also lived at Whitebrook, where Ian McLean was head trainer. "You guys ready to go to the caroling party?" Samantha asked. "It's almost eight o'clock." Ashleigh's parents, Derek and Elaine Griffen, had a farm not far away. Tonight they were holding a big Christmas party.

"Wow!" Ashleigh said on seeing the younger woman's green velvet party dress. "You look fantastic! That green really sets off your hair."

Smiling, Samantha tossed her long red curls dramatically. "Thanks. You look great too."

Ashleigh patted her tummy under her dark red maternity dress. "At eight months pregnant, I don't know how great I look." Privately, she thought she looked like a big red birthday balloon in this outfit.

Instantly Mike enclosed Ashleigh in a quick hug. "You've never looked better, and you know it."

Ashleigh kissed Mike on the cheek and saw Samantha grin. The Griffens, Reeses, and McLeans had known each other for years—ever since Ashleigh's parents and Ian McLean had worked to-

2

gether at Townsend Acres, one of the biggest and most prestigious training and breeding outfits in Kentucky. In fact, Clay Townsend, owner of Townsend Acres, owned half of Wonder and all her offspring.

"Where's Tor tonight?" Ashleigh asked.

"With his father. We agreed that we'd each spend tonight with our families and then see each other tomorrow." Tor Nelson and Samantha had been a steady couple for ages.

Soon Ashleigh, Mike, and Samantha were joined by Mike's father, Ian and Beth McLean, and Len, the old black stable manager. Samantha's father, Ian, had married Beth Raines a few years earlier. Just a month before, they had joyfully announced Beth's pregnancy.

"Hello, Shining girl," Samantha said, scratching the elegant roan filly behind the ears. Shining, who belonged to Samantha, was a half sister to Wonder.

"And here's Fleet Goddess. Hello, sweetie," Ashleigh said, giving her treats. "You don't have long to go now either, huh? I know how you feel." Fleet Goddess was in foal again, as was Wonder. Sometime in the early spring, both mares would have their foals. Just thinking about it made a shiver go down Ashleigh's spine. To her mind, there was nothing more miraculous than a newborn foal. She could hardly wait to introduce her own child to all the marvels of the farm. *Just one more month*, she thought.

As a professional jockey, Ashleigh had always had a lean, tightly muscled figure. Now, nearing the end of her pregnancy, she felt uncharacteristically awkward and a little unwieldy as she crossed the snowy path. Although she was thrilled and excited about the baby, part of her knew that she would be glad to be back in the saddle again once the baby was born. It had been very hard not to be able to ride a horse for the past several months.

"Hey there, Blues King," Mike said, giving the racer part of an apple. The Thoroughbred stallion lipped it up, then bobbed his head as if to say, "Thank you."

Ashleigh, Samantha, and the others moved down the aisle, saying hello to the young horses just starting training and those who were already well into their racing careers. The stable had been decorated with evergreen wreaths and red velvet bows. Ashleigh breathed deeply, taking in the Christmassy scent of pine needles mixed with fresh hay and horses.

Then she and Samantha stepped down a few stairs, leaving the men engrossed in a conversation about the upcoming spring training schedule.

At the next stall a tall, slender filly was waiting. "Hi, Precocious," Ashleigh crooned, rubbing the filly's gleaming black head. Precocious, the daughter of Fleet Goddess and Jazzman, two more of Whitebrook's former champions, was doing well in training.

4

Samantha joined her at the stall. "She's really beautiful, isn't she?"

Nodding, Ashleigh said, "We just might have a winner in her." It was an exciting prospect.

Beside Precocious in the next stall was Mr. Wonderful, another son of Wonder. Like his mother, he was a rich chestnut color with a white star on his forehead.

"Yes, you can have an apple," Ashleigh said with a chuckle, giving one to the colt. He gave a small, excited neigh before crunching the apple happily.

Behind the women a horse snorted. Turning around, Ashleigh noticed one of Mike's geldings stepping anxiously around his stall.

"Hey there, fella. What's the matter?" Ashleigh said softly. The large horse bobbed his head and pushed against his stall door. His eyes were wide and rolling from side to side as he looked around nervously.

"Something's upsetting him," Samantha said, unlatching the stall door.

"I'll check." Without giving it a second thought, Ashleigh slipped inside the stall, took the horse's halter, and spoke soothingly to him. Then she glanced around the stall. "I don't see anything—oh, wait—there's something . . ."

As Ashleigh frowned into the dim light at the back of the stall, she noticed a rustling in the clean straw bedding on the floor. Suddenly a tiny brown mouse darted out and scampered across the floor. The horse snorted and pulled hard on his halter, but Ashleigh held him firmly.

"It's a mouse—" she began, then everything seemed to happen at once. One of the stable cats shot through the open stall door to leap on the mouse, which quickly dove into the thick straw. The cat furiously began scrabbling in the straw, and it was too much for the high-strung racer. With a whinny of fear, he ripped his halter out of Ashleigh's hand and lunged out the stall door, nearly running Samantha down. But the younger woman had been confronted with runaway horses before and she instinctively grabbed his halter again, though the horse tried to rear.

Ashleigh rushed out of the stall to help before the horse hurt himself or Samantha. Scared now, and panicking in his fear, the horse kicked out with his back hooves and caught Ashleigh squarely in the side with a powerful thrust. She fell backward, and a shock of pain exploded through her body. With a low groan, she collapsed on the floor and rolled up into a ball, clutching her stomach.

"Ashleigh!" she heard Samantha scream, but she had no breath to answer.

She heard Mike cry out and run down the aisle, and then he was beside her, shielding her with his body as he yelled for help. Opening her eyes, trying to catch her breath, Ashleigh could see that Len and Mr. McLean were already at the horse's head, grabbing his halter. They quickly led the horse down the aisle and away from the action that had frightened him so. Then Ashleigh was aware of Samantha dropping to her knees beside her, looking white with fear. For long minutes Ashleigh lay on the cold, smooth cement of the stable floor, her face twisted with pain, her arms wrapped around her wide belly as if she were protecting her baby. She struggled to gasp in a breath, but it felt as though every bit of air had been knocked out of her.

"It's okay, Ash, honey—you're going to be okay," Mike said hoarsely. Turning around, he bit out, "Call an ambulance. Let's get her to the hospital."

"No," Ashleigh managed to gasp. Already the shock of the kick was receding, and she took in a ragged breath. "No—no, just take me back to the house for now." She looked up to see frantic worry etched across Mike's face. She didn't want to add to it. Maybe she was fine. Maybe the baby was fine.

Without hesitation he scooped her up into his arms and headed for the main farmhouse he and Ashleigh shared with his father. The cold air went right through Ashleigh, and she felt herself start to shiver. Inside the farmhouse Mike set her gently on the couch in the living room, then examined her face anxiously. She tried to smile up at him, but her whole body trembled.

"Do you think anything's broken?"

Ashleigh lay back against the pillows, feeling the house's warmth begin to seep into her bones. Her stomach already hurt much less, and she clasped her hands around the hard mound of the baby. "No." She shook her head. "I feel much better." She managed a weak smile. "I just got the wind knocked out of me, that's all."

"How's the baby?" Tenderly Mike touched her side.

"I think it's okay. I just want to lie here for a moment." The others bustled in and Samantha rushed to Ashleigh's side. "Oh, Ash—it was all my fault! I never should have let you go in there." Turning to Mike, she asked, "Have you called the doctor?"

"Not yet." Mike squeezed Ashleigh's hand, and she gripped back, grateful that he was there.

"I'm okay, really," she tried to reassure Samantha. "It wasn't your fault—it just happened." At seeing her friend's worried face, Ashleigh said, "Maybe a cup of tea would be nice."

Samantha whirled and headed for the kitchen, looking thankful for something to do.

Ashleigh made herself smile again at Mike. "I feel much better," she insisted.

"Well, I still think we should call the doctor, just to be on the safe side."

A few minutes later, when Mike finally reached the doctor's office, Ashleigh had to admit that something was wrong. Her body shook with fear. She was almost certain she was experiencing the contractions of premature labor.

Several hours later, Mike came out of the waiting room at Lexington Memorial Hospital to let their friends and family know what was happening. He took a deep breath—his mind was still reeling from the shock of everything happening so quickly. His thoughts were on Ashleigh, down the hall in the delivery room.

As he entered the waiting room Mrs. Griffen rushed up to him and was joined quickly by Samantha.

"They haven't been able to stop the labor," Mike said quietly, feeling as though his heart were pounding right out of his chest. "They're just going to let the baby come now." He struggled to think of something positive to say. "Dr. Maystrom said that since Ash was already eight months along, the baby should be okay. Lots of babies are born premature and have no problems. And the kick didn't break any bones or anything."

Her face pale, Mrs. Griffen nodded and gripped his hand in silent support. Swallowing hard, trying to keep a brave face, Mike looked around the waiting room, taking in the concerned faces of all the people who loved Ashleigh. Ashleigh's parents were there, and her sister Caroline and her husband, and her younger brother, Rory, had been notified. Samantha was there, and so were Ian and Beth. Mike's father, Gene Reese, was sitting next to Len, twisting his cap in his hands.

They all sat waiting silently, hoping and praying for the best.

"I've got to go back now," Mike said, motioning toward the door. They nodded. Mrs. Griffen kissed him, and then he headed back down the hall where Ashleigh was about to give birth to their child.

It was toward dawn on Christmas Day when Mike pushed his way through the swinging double doors again. As before, everyone crowded around him, anxious for news. Mrs. Griffen on one side, his father on the other, each took his hands in support. He felt numb, full of sorrow. Now he'd have to give Ashleigh's parents the news, and he didn't know how they would take it.

"How is she?" Mrs. Griffen said, her voice breaking.

"The baby was born about an hour ago," Mike said dully. "It's a girl." Remembering the newborn's small, red face and perfect fingers, he managed a feeble smile. "She's tiny, but beautiful. But she's having trouble breathing on her own, so she's in an oxygen tent. Nobody can see her yet."

10

He heard Samantha bite back a cry. "And—Ashleigh?" she whispered.

This was the hard part. Inside, his heart felt as though it were made of lead. Mike looked at them, at everyone who had stayed through the long night wanting to help, waiting for news. "Ash," he began hoarsely, "had some trouble during the delivery. Her . . . blood pressure shot up. I'm not really sure exactly what happened . . . but the doctor said it made a tiny blood vessel burst in her brain."

Next to Mike, Mrs. Griffen went white and sagged against him. Her husband put his arm around her and helped her stand.

"My little girl," Mrs. Griffen whispered.

Mike was aware of the slow trickle of tears down Samantha's face.

"She's—" Again Mike's voice broke, and he could feel hot tears welling up in his eyes. The thought of Ashleigh, whom he loved more than anything, being in danger was almost more than he could bear. He felt if he didn't get out of there fast, he would just fall apart. He had to get back to her side, be with her. "She's drifting in and out of consciousness. They've taken her to the intensive-care unit. Dr. Maystrom says the next twelve hours will tell whether she'll . . . recover or not. They've got a neurologist looking at her." He rubbed his hand against his eyes.

"Can we see her?" Mr. Griffen asked quietly.

"Only one person is allowed in her room," Mike said hesitantly.

"You stay with her, Mike," Mrs. Griffen said at once. "Give her our love and our prayers."

Mike nodded, and with a last glance into the faces of friends and family, he turned and pushed through the doors again, rushing to be at Ashleigh's side.

Ashleigh was conscious of feeling cold and tired. She felt as though she were floating in a cold tank of water, except that her body felt so heavy, she knew she would just sink to the bottom.

Where was she? What was going on? She couldn't remember what had happened. *I have to open my eyes,* she thought. *I have to see what's happening. I have to find Mike.* But even though she tried hard and concentrated, she couldn't seem to make her eyes open. She was so tired. Maybe if she rested awhile, she would feel better.

Then she felt someone take her cold hand. She smiled. She would recognize Mike's touch anywhere. His warm, work-roughened hand felt like a jolt of life against her cool skin. Her heart lightened as she heard his soft voice floating toward her.

"You're going to be okay, sweetie," he said. "Do you hear me? You're going to be okay. You have to be, Ash. I can't do it without you."

Again she tried to open her eyes. Yes! They

opened a slit, even though Ashleigh felt as though there were heavy weights trying to hold them closed.

"Where am I?" she tried to whisper, but no sound came out. She realized there was a plastic tube in the back of her throat. It hurt when she swallowed. She tried to look around, first fastening on Mike's dear, familiar face, looking so pale and worried above her. All around her, machines softly beeped, hummed, and clicked. Turning her head with great effort, she saw the faintest bit of sunlight creeping through the slit of the window curtains. It was morning. It was Christmas Day.

"You're in the hospital, sweetie," Mike answered. "You got kicked by a horse, remember?" A solitary tear rolled down Mike's handsome face, and he dashed it away with the back of his hand.

"What about the baby?" she managed to croak. Ashleigh was feeling weaker by the moment, but all she could think of was her baby. Dimly she remembered the wrenching pain of contractions, an operating room, nurses and doctors scurrying around . . .

"The baby's fine," Mike told her. "She's beautiful. Now you just have to get better so you can help me take care of her, okay?"

Closing her eyes for a moment, Ashleigh smiled faintly. She was so tired, she really had to rest. She had to rest up so that she would have the strength to see her baby. In her mind, she had a sudden image of a small, sweet face, looking very solemn and very pink. "Oh, Mike, I saw her," Ashleigh whispered. "She's so beautiful. She looks just like you. She'll be okay, Mike, I know she will." Ashleigh's body ached and felt heavy and still. Her throat hurt more now. She felt herself slipping away into a sweet unconsciousness where there was no pain and no worry. Before her, she could see her daughter's small face. Mike was holding her. They were both dressed in white and were standing in a big, open field. *How funny*, she thought. "You'll be okay, too," she breathed.

Dimly, as though from a great distance, she could hear Mike's voice. "Ash! Ash, honey! Please don't go, don't leave me!"

From where she lay, Ashleigh tried to tell him not to worry, but she couldn't get the words out. She couldn't even open her eyes. Then she was looking down on Mike from above, and she saw how he was resting his head against her and calling her name. "Don't worry, darling," she wanted to say. "There's nothing to worry about anymore. Take care of Christina. Take care of our beautiful daughter." Ashleigh felt tired, so tired. All she wanted to do was sleep. A tiny smile curved the corners of her mouth. Christina . . . her beautiful daughter, Christina.

Part One

1

ONE, TWO, THREE, SQUEEZE . . . IT TOOK ALL OF CHRISTINA'S concentration to keep her Welsh pony, Triumph, in a collected canter as they headed for the jump. Mentally she counted his strides as they rode toward the brush, being careful to keep her body in a straight line from head to hip to foot. Shoulders back, eyes forward, a smooth line formed by the reins held firmly in her hands, Christina counted strides and squeezed her calves to give Triumph the signal to jump. Effortlessly the pony sailed over the hurdle, his dainty hooves not even touching the row of plastic bushes on top.

After the brush would come a parallel, then a gate. Earlier that morning Christina had walked the large outdoor course and had already calculated her approach to each obstacle. The last jump would be a combination—the biggest one she had tried yet—and she knew she had to give Triumph a small extra stride if he was to be in perfect position when they were upon the jump.

At ten, Christina Reese had been taking jumping lessons from Tor and Samantha Nelson at their stable in Lexington for as long as she could remember. After all, she had been on horses practically since she was a baby. Since her mother had died when she was born, Christina had spent a great deal of time with her father as he worked. She remembered sitting in front of him in the saddle on one of his Thoroughbred racers when she was barely two. And she'd had her own very small Shetland pony, Daisy, by the time she was four.

The early April air brushed softly against her face as Christina and Triumph flew over the large combination. Automatically she gave the pony the extra rein he needed to stretch out over the jump. Then the course was completed, and Christina could breathe again. Slowing Triumph down, she trotted over to where Tor and Samantha were waiting.

The smiles on their faces told her she had done well, and she felt a rush of pleasure.

"That was terrific, Chris!" Samantha cried, coming to hold Triumph's bridle so Christina could dismount.

"Well done. Your timing and seat were perfect almost the whole way through," Tor praised her.

"Thanks," Christina said, smiling. She took off

her hard hat and brushed her blond bangs out of her eyes. "Triumph is a great pony, aren't you, boy?" Turning around, she rubbed his soft warm nose and hugged him around the neck.

"Why don't you get this guy cooled out," Samantha suggested, flipping her red braid over her shoulder. "Your dad will be here to pick you up in a little while."

"Okay." Christina led Triumph out of the training oval and down a wide hall to the stabling area. The Nelsons' training stable was one of her favorite places, and the Nelsons were two of her favorite people. Samantha and Tor were good friends of her father and had also been close to Christina's mother, Ashleigh. Christina loved to hear them talk about her mother.

From the time she was very small, Christina had always felt different because she had no mother. She knew her father was the best father in the world, and she adored him completely. But there was a constant ache inside her, a loneliness that only a real mother could heal.

Fortunately Christina had been surrounded all her life by people who had loved her mother and loved to talk about her. Ashleigh Griffen had been a famous jockey, and all over the house there were pictures of her, some on horseback in her jockey's silks, some standing in front of a horse in the winner's circle at a race, and some just taken casually at home in the living room or the kitchen. There were even videos of her winning races on her Thoroughbreds, having a birthday party, getting married to Christina's father. These things had made Christina feel close to the mother who was no longer there, and had given her a bond to the special woman whom so many people had loved, who had worked miracles with her Thoroughbreds, and whom Christina had never known. Christina pretended to talk to her mother in her mind, just telling her what was going on, how she felt about things. Sometimes she was sure her mother could hear her.

But even though Christina could talk to her mother that way, there were still times when she needed a real person to turn to. Samantha Nelson was just about the most important person in Christina's life, besides her father.

Until she'd married Tor, Samantha had also lived at Whitebrook, in the small cottage her father, Ian McLean, shared with his wife, Beth, and their son, Kevin, who was several months younger than Christina. While Christina's grandfather, Gene Reese, was alive, Ian McLean had been Whitebrook's head trainer. But several years after Gene's death, Christina's father had made Mr. McLean his partner.

In some ways Samantha had been like a surrogate mother to Christina. Besides just helping her with her riding skills, Samantha had always been there to confide in and lend Christina guidance and support. The best thing was that Samantha told Christina she was a natural horsewoman, just like Christina's mother had been, and that made Christina prouder than anything else. Her greatest wish was to someday, somehow live up to her mother's accomplishments and to have her father be as proud of her as he was of her mother. It was a goal she worked toward daily with all of her practices, her lessons, her training.

After walking Triumph up and down in the stable yard for a while, Christina led him back inside and groomed him thoroughly. The bay Welsh pony, with his sturdy legs shading into black and his powerful neck gleaming from exercise, stood patiently as Christina picked his hooves and brushed out his mane.

"You're such a good boy," Christina told him. "You were wonderful today."

Triumph bobbed his head as though to say, "I know."

As Christina worked, several other riders came to collect their horses. Some only boarded their horses or ponies at the Nelsons', but others took lessons in either show-jumping or steeplechasing.

"Hi, Chris," Jo Ellen Marks said, taking out her pony and putting him in crossties so she could saddle him.

"Hi, Jo Ellen. Going out on the trails?"

"Yep. We're working on building his stamina."

20

Jo Ellen was two years older than Christina, and her pony was as big as a pony could be and still be classified a pony—about fourteen hands high. Christina knew Jo Ellen and Scotch had been working toward competing in three-day eventing. In some ways, the three-day event was just about the hardest equestrian sport to compete in. Riders and their mounts had to perform in dressage, cross-country riding, and show-jumping. It was very difficult to do all three things well.

Lately Christina had been thinking about training for three-day eventing herself. Did she have what it took? Up until now, she had been focusing only on show-jumping. She frowned, rubbing Triumph's bay coat smooth. She was only ten years old, but she knew that soon she would outgrow the stout little pony. If she was going to continue riding seriously, she would need a different mount. "I don't want to give you up, Triumph," she whispered against his warm side.

An older girl, Mandy Jarvis, came to get her horse from its stall. Mandy was one of the best riders Tor and Samantha had ever taught. Mandy's horse, Bright Star, was one of Shining's offspring. Everyone knew Shining was Samantha's favorite broodmare and had been a very successful flat racer until retiring about seven years before. Now the black girl tacked up Bright Star and led the roan Thoroughbred filly down the aisle.

21

"Hi, Mandy," Christina said, currying Triumph's side.

"Oh, hey there, Christina," Mandy said, a smile lighting her pretty face. As usual, her thick black hair was in a tight French braid and her riding outfit was impeccable. Christina thought Mandy looked exactly how a horsewoman should look—tall, slim, and elegant. It was hard to believe that when Mandy had been a little girl, she had been in a car accident that had left her in leg braces for almost two years. Now she walked and rode perfectly.

"I almost didn't see you behind Triumph. How was your lesson today?" Mandy asked.

"Tor and Sammy seemed to think it went pretty well," Christina said modestly. "Are you here for the advanced?"

"Yeah. I just want to brush up on my form so I'll be ready for the show at Haversham next weekend."

Christina smiled. Mandy Jarvis had perfect form—it didn't need any brushing up. But she knew the older girl was almost obsessive about riding her best. Christina had heard rumors that Tor was urging Mandy to try out for the U.S. Olympic Equestrian Team in a few years.

Just then Samantha poked her head around the corner. "Chris! Your dad's here!"

"Coming!" Christina answered. After unhooking Triumph from his crossties, she led him down the aisle to his stall. Once he was inside, she made sure he had a full hay net and fresh water in his bucket. With a final hug and a kiss on his soft nose, Christina tore herself away and headed into the stable yard.

Her father was just parking the familiar Whitebrook pickup truck. He swung out of the driver's seat and came to hug Christina. "Hi, sweetie," he said. "How was class?"

"Pretty good. Tor said I had an almost perfect seat."

"Good for you." Mike Reese smiled down at his daughter and brushed a lock of her hair off her cheek. She had gotten her sunlit blond hair from him, but her hazel eyes were exactly like her mother's.

Samantha walked up and greeted Christina's dad.

"I'm glad you're here, Sammy," he said. "I have something to tell both of you."

Her father looked very serious, and his face looked tired. "Dad, what's the matter?" Christina urged.

"It's Fleet Goddess."

Fleet Goddess, a horse that Christina's mother had purchased as a filly, was now one of Whitebrook's best broodmares. Since she had retired, she had foaled ten beautiful sons and daughters. Christina had been looking forward to the birth of her latest foal. "What's wrong with Goddess?"

Samantha asked, concern in her voice. When Samantha had been only a few years older than Christina was now, she had taken special care of Fleet Goddess and helped her become a winning racer. Christina knew there was still a strong bond between them.

"She's been in labor since early this morning, and it isn't going well," Mr. Reese said tersely.

"Since this morning? I didn't notice anything," Christina said in confusion. But then, she had only quickly kissed the mare on her way out to class after mucking out her share of the stalls in the mares' barn. She felt a pang of guilt as she remembered stopping by several of the other mares' stalls—the ones who'd already had their foals. Christina loved watching the tiny colts and fillies as they discovered the world around them. But she hadn't spent any time with Goddess.

"What do you mean, not going well?" Samantha asked. There were lines of worry around her eyes, and her mouth looked pinched.

"Dr. Mendez has been with her for a few hours, and he's getting concerned. The labor is taking too long, and Fleet Goddess is getting tired. She also seems to have come down with a sudden virus. Anyway, I want to hurry back home."

Christina headed for the truck, and Samantha headed for the stable office. "I'm coming with you," she said. "Let me just tell Tor."

Twenty minutes later Christina's father pulled the truck onto the long gravel driveway at White-brook. Spring flowers were in bloom along the stone paths leading to all the buildings. The blanket of winter snow had long since melted, and the rolling fields and paddocks were mantled in crisp green grass and clover. White slat fences surrounded the paddocks, and sleek Thoroughbreds were grazing in the mild spring air. The main farmhouse where Christina and her father lived had been freshly painted and looked tidy and clean in the bright sunlight.

But Christina hardly noticed the welcoming familiarity of the farm. She and Samantha were sitting on the edge of the seat, and as soon as her dad pulled to a stop they unsnapped their seat belts and leaped out to run to the weathered mares' barn.

Christina reached the barn first and darted into the large, clean building. Stalls on both sides formed a wide middle aisle, and Christina headed down it with her father and Samantha on her heels. In seconds they were at Fleet Goddess's stall. Besides the vet, Dr. Mendez, Ian and Kevin McLean were there.

Christina and Kevin McLean had grown up together and shared the easy familiarity and rivalry of siblings. While both of them loved horses, Kevin was more interested in flat racing and Christina in jumping. Now Kevin came forward, a solemn look on his freckled face.

"Hey, Chris, Sammy," he said in a low voice.

Samantha kissed him, then asked, "How is she?"

Kevin frowned. He shared his half sister, Samantha's, coloring of red hair, green eyes, and fair skin, and Christina often thought that they had similar expressions as well. "Not good," he admitted now. "Your dad told Dr. Mendez to focus on saving Goddess and worry about the foal later."

Christina put her hand to her mouth. Until this moment the thought that either Goddess or the foal might die hadn't occurred to her. Now it made her feel sick. One look at Samantha's face told her that she was feeling the same.

Hesitantly Christina walked over to the roomy box stall reserved for laboring mothers, but her father shook his head when she tried to get closer. "We need to keep her calm," he said softly. "And Dr. Mendez has his hands full."

Then Fleet Goddess let out an anguished groan. Christina trembled at the sound of one of her beloved horses in pain.

"Mike," Samantha said tautly, her face white with fear, "isn't there anything we can do?"

Looking upset himself, Christina's father answered, "Right now it's a waiting game, Sammy. But we're going to try our best to save them both. You know we will."

"Can I go in? Maybe I could . . . hold her head," Samantha suggested desperately. "She knows me and trusts me. Maybe I could help."

Christina's father came over and patted Samantha's back. "I know how you feel, Sammy, and I know how much Goddess means to you. But I think right now we should leave Dr. Mendez alone so he can do his job. You know he's the best in the business, right?"

Miserably, Samantha nodded.

Then another low, pained groan came from the stall, and Christina gasped. The sound almost tore her heart in two. She felt so helpless! She couldn't bear to hear Goddess in pain—she just couldn't bear it! Whirling, she ran down the middle aisle and burst through the door to the sunlight outside. She had to get away. If she couldn't help Goddess, if there was nothing she could do, then she didn't want to be there.

2

CHRISTINA POUNDED ACROSS THE STABLE YARD AND headed for her special spot behind the farmhouse. She had found it when she was very young, and ever since then, she had gone there when she needed to think. She flew past the ancient, gnarled apple trees that were covered with sweetly scented tiny white blossoms. Then, behind the oldest tree at the edge of the yard, right where the yard ended and the woods began, she flung herself down and began to weep.

"Oh, Goddess," she choked out through her tears, "please be okay. I don't want anything to happen to you."

Then she felt a cool hand brushing the hair off her face, and Samantha's arms gathered her up and wrapped around her in a comforting hug.

"Shh, shh," she murmured, stroking Christina's

hair. "I know how you're feeling. But we just have to wait and see and hope for the best."

"I'm so worried," Christina sobbed. "Goddess can't die! She just can't! And neither can the foal," she added fiercely. Somehow, knowing that her own mother had owned and loved Fleet Goddess made it that much more unbearable for Christina to lose the mare. She couldn't explain it.

Samantha held her while she cried, and after several minutes the tears slowed, then stopped. Christina rested against her, sniffling occasionally.

"I can't stand it when bad things happen," she said finally.

"I know, sweetie," Samantha said, her own voice sounding shaky. "It's really hard sometimes. When something awful happens, it can be so hard to see beyond it, to know that you have to go on no matter what. Even if you feel like you can't."

Christina sat quietly for a while. She knew that Samantha was talking about more than Goddess. She was talking about Christina's mother, too. Christina knew how hard it had been for everyone on the farm when Ashleigh died. Of course they didn't think that things would ever be the same. But life went on, as Samantha said. It was something to think about.

Christina wiped her eyes and tried to smile. "Maybe we should go back to the house for something to drink. It'll give us something to do until Dad tells us the news."

"Good idea," Samantha said. She stood up, took Christina's hand, and pulled her to a standing position. Then, still holding hands, they headed for the farmhouse.

In the kitchen Christina sat at the table and wiped her eyes with a paper napkin. Samantha busied herself making iced tea, then poured two tall glasses and sat down beside Christina.

"We have to hope for the best," Samantha repeated firmly.

"Right," Christina said, trying to sound brave. "Maybe everything will be okay. We just have to wait and see."

"After all, nothing's happened yet," Samantha said. "Remember what happened with your mother and Wonder?"

Christina nodded. Wonder was one of the oldest horses at Whitebrook. When Wonder had first been born, no one thought she would live. Christina's mother, Ashleigh, had saved the filly, and they had gone on to win the Kentucky Derby and many other championship races together. Christina had heard the story many times, about how Ashleigh had had to fight to keep the filly and had more than once convinced Mr. Townsend not to sell her. Against all odds, Wonder had become a champion, and it had all been due to Ashleigh's determination.

"That was before my dad and I went to Townsend Acres," Samantha said, taking a sip of her iced tea. "But I heard about it later, and then Ashleigh and I used to talk about it." Samantha smiled at Christina. "When I first came to Townsend Acres, my own mom had just died. But you know about that. Anyway, Ashleigh took me under her wing and helped convince my dad to let me ride again."

Christina knew that Samantha's mother had died in a riding accident.

"Anyway, I felt like my life was starting over again, with Ashleigh's friendship. And watching her around the farm helped me focus on my own dreams of being a trainer. Your mom loved her Thoroughbreds so much, and they loved her. I used to tease her about being part horse herself. She was a really special person. I remember thinking her horses would do anything for her—she brought out the best in them."

Christina tried to smile. "Someday I'd like to do that."

"Someday you will, sweetie," Samantha said.

It was almost dinnertime when Mike Reese came into the farmhouse kitchen. He looked tired, and his jeans were dirty from kneeling on the barn floor.

"Dad! How is she? And how's the foal?" Christina asked instantly.

"The foal was born—a filly," he said, sitting down

31

at the table. "Goddess had a bad time of it. She's showing signs of a weird systemic infection. It must have come on during the night, but I've never seen anything act so quickly. We have her back in her own stall and on intravenous antibiotics."

"Oh, Mike," Samantha said softly. "What does Dr. Mendez say?"

"It's touch and go."

Christina bit down on her lip, hard.

Then he continued, "If she improves, it will be within the next two days. We'll just have to keep pumping medicine into her and hope."

"I'll go out to see her in a minute. How's the filly?" Samantha asked.

"Not very good," Christina's dad admitted. "She's a full-term foal but small, and she seems very weakened by the long and difficult birth. And of course Goddess won't be able to nurse her. Her milk will be dry by the time the mare is on her feet again."

"Yes, but we can bottle-feed her," Samantha said, a determined note in her voice.

"We can, but . . . well, I just don't think the foal's going to make it. Dr. Mendez is doing blood tests on her now to see if she's got the same virus that Goddess has. If she does . . ."

Christina knew it was very dangerous for a newborn to get ill before it had had a chance to build up its natural immunity. "Also," he continued, "the foal's fetlocks are deformed. She'll never be a pleasure horse, much less a racer. I mean, I hope the filly makes it, but right now I have to concentrate on getting Goddess through the night."

"Dad! You can't just let the foal die!" Christina grabbed her father's arm and stared up into his face. All her earlier fears rushed back, and she felt her throat constrict.

"Sweetie, I want to save this foal as much as you do—but she's had a real bad time of it. I'd be surprised if we could even get her to drink from a bottle," he said softly. "Of course we'll try, but we have to be practical, too."

"No, we don't! We don't have to be practical. All we *have* to do is save Goddess and her filly!" Christina tore herself from her father's arms and burst out the kitchen door to run to the mares' barn.

Inside the barn, Dr. Mendez was washing his hands at the sink at the front of the building.

"Where's Goddess?" Christina asked, quickly wiping her eyes.

"She's resting in her stall," the vet told her gently. "Why don't you wait awhile to see her? It's best that she just sleep right now."

Christina's jaw set stubbornly as she began to consider ways to see the mare. She had to see her, make sure that she was still alive and was going to stay alive. But there was also the foal to consider.

Dr. Mendez dried his hands on a paper towel and said, "I have something else to show you, though. Follow me."

Christina's eyebrows shot up. "The foal?" she said excitedly, hurrying down the aisle after the vet. One of the day hands had just finished forking out all the soiled straw and replacing it with fresh-smelling clean bedding. Christina leaned against the open stall door. Len, her father's old stable manager, was in the stall. Her eyes widened, and she gasped.

There, right next to Len, was a very small foal. It had fuzzy, jet-black hair and large brown eyes. An odd, lopsided white splotch covered one ear and part of her head. But the foal was standing up!

"Yep, I was surprised too," Dr. Mendez confirmed. "After all she's been through and with the problems she has, I expected her to curl up on the straw and not move again."

"I stayed with the filly," Len said, "when they went to attend to Goddess. I dried her off and made her comfortable . . ." He gave the small foal an affectionate look. "And they came back to find this little miss on her feet."

Slowly Christina entered the stall, being careful not to alarm the tiny foal. Behind her she heard footsteps, and then both her father's and Samantha's muffled cries of surprise.

The newborn filly, having no inborn fear of humans, watched Christina alertly with her large, wide brown eyes. Her two tiny ears, one black, one white, were pricked forward with curiosity.

"She has weird coloring for a Thoroughbred," Christina said, smiling at the undersize foal.

As she studied the tiny filly, she noticed that the foal's front legs were deformed. Her forelegs bent in at an awkward angle, so that the tiny ankles almost touched the ground. The hind legs looked normal.

Dr. Mendez joined Christina and Len and gently stroked his hand down the filly's back. "I've seen this before in foals—usually the back legs are affected too. Sometimes it's genetic, but sometimes it's just caused by how they were curled up in their dam's womb."

"Will she live? Can I bottle-feed her?" It took all of Christina's nerve to ask those questions. She didn't know what she would do if the vet said no. But she couldn't let the filly die—she just couldn't! Not when the little horse was standing up so bravely, all by herself in this big empty stall. She knew her mother, Ashleigh, would have felt the same way.

"What do you think, Bill?" Mr. Reese asked, coming to stand beside them. "I thought this filly was in a bad way."

"I thought so too," the vet agreed. "Until I turned my back and she stood up." He smiled at Christina.

"Now I'd say she's got a fighting chance."

"What about her legs?" Christina's father asked.

"Well," Dr. Mendez said, "if it's genetic, there's nothing we can do. But if it's just developmental weakness . . . there is something you could try."

"Dad, we have to," Christina insisted, touching the filly softly, feeling the tiny ribs beneath the small damp sides. "Don't you see? We have to." Looking deeply into the foal's eyes, Christina sent her a message: *We're going to save you. I'm going to take care of you. Don't be afraid.*

"It's a shame we don't have a nursing mare available. But she should do okay on a milk substitute. I guess I better go mix some up, then," her father said. "Sammy, want to come with me? You can sterilize the bottles. And you better call that husband of yours and tell him what's happening."

"Someone has to nurse the filly every two hours, round the clock, for several weeks," Dr. Mendez pointed out.

"I can do it!" Christina said firmly. "I know I can."

"What about school?" her dad asked.

"I can help," Samantha said instantly.

"So can I," Kevin McLean said, suddenly appearing in the aisle.

"I reckon I can find some time, too," Len allowed with a wide grin, standing behind Kevin. Christina knew there would be no way to keep him from nursing the foal.

36

Slowly her father looked at the faces around him. Then, with a glance at Christina, he said, "You're certainly your mother's daughter. She wouldn't have let me give up either."

"Then we'll try?" Christina cried excitedly.

"Of course we'll try. Just look at her." Christina's father pointed to the filly, who was still gazing up at them with wide, trusting eyes.

Samantha laughed. "I'd say she looks hungry already. Let's get that formula mixed."

Christina's dad turned serious and said, "Chris, it's possible we won't be able to fix the filly's legs. You realize that, right?"

Christina set her chin stubbornly. "We can fix them."

"I want you to tell me you understand that this filly might not make it—even with all your care and wishes and hope. Okay?"

Frowning at the ground, Christina muttered, "I understand."

"All right, then. I'll be back in a minute with a couple of baby bottles. We'll try feeding her right after dinner."

"She's so small," Rebecca Morrison said, peeking through the slats on the stable door. Christina's best friend and fellow horse lover had come over to help take care of the newborn foal.

Christina had just finished giving the filly her first

feeding. It had taken almost two hours to get one bottle of milk into her. It wasn't that she was too weak to suckle or uninterested in feeding: she simply didn't know what to do. Christina and Kevin had taken turns wetting their fingers with the milk and touching it to the filly's lips. Finally the filly had understood and latched on to the bottle's nipple firmly. After she'd gotten the hang of it, she'd drained a whole bottle in no time. Christina and Rebecca would have no trouble bottle-feeding her later.

"Yeah, but the vet doesn't think she's premature. Help me push this bale of hay over, okay?"

The two girls had gotten Christina's dad's permission to sleep in the mares' barn that night so they could stay close to the filly. Now they were arranging their sleeping bags on top of a line of hay bales. Rebecca set up her portable radio and tuned it softly to a popular station.

"How was your lesson today?" Rebecca asked.

This morning's jumping lesson felt as if it had happened years ago. Christina thought back. "Pretty good. But I think I'm going to need another pony soon."

Rebecca nodded in understanding. "Last week I noticed that your legs are starting to hang down pretty far. I'm lucky that I started on a big pony myself." Rebecca's pony, Maxie, still suited her fine. She grinned. "Maybe you won't grow much this summer."

Before Christina could say anything, Kevin came into the barn, followed by Dr. Mendez.

"Hi, girls," the vet said. "Gather round, and let me explain what's going to happen. Here are the special boots for the filly."

He held up a pair of tiny leather boots that looked very similar to the shin guards horses sometimes wore to protect their legs. Rows of leather straps and buckles fastened the boots at the back. Crossing to where the filly lay curled on the straw, the vet gently flexed one of her forelegs.

"These little boots will, I hope, gradually and gently help her fetlocks straighten out and become strong. I doubt that the problem is genetic, since her dam and sire have had quite a few perfect foals. In about four to six months, if all goes well, her legs should look pretty normal."

Christina watched as the vet carefully fit a leather boot around the filly's leg. It went almost from hoof to knee. The little foal didn't seem to like it and clumsily tried to pull away. But in the end both boots were on.

"As she grows we'll have to get larger boots, of course," Dr. Mendez explained. "Now, she should wear the boots four hours on and one hour off, to start. Make sure the boots are clean and dry and that they're not rubbing sores into her legs."

"Got it," Christina said.

"Good girl. I'm going to give the filly some extra

shots, vitamins and stuff. You guys make sure you disinfect everything around her, especially these bottles."

After giving the foal her shots, Dr. Mendez went to check on Fleet Goddess, who was resting in her stall. Christina had gone to check on her earlier and to assure her that her foal was doing all right. As soon as Fleet Goddess recovered, they would try to put mother and foal back together again.

Kevin McLean left around nine o'clock, and Mr. Reese arrived to check on the girls.

Christina had just started to feed the filly again. This time the foal knew exactly what to do, and with a lunge she fastened her mouth around the bottle's nipple. In moments she was sucking hard, gulping down the milk. Laughing, Christina held up the bottle so the filly wouldn't swallow air.

"Well, I'll be," her dad said wonderingly.

"This is her second bottle," Rebecca told him proudly.

"Dad, we have to name the filly," Christina reminded him, watching as the milk level in the bottle got lower and lower.

"Hmm, I guess we do. Got any ideas?" he asked.

"I know—why not name her Determined, or something like that, because she's gone through so much just to get this far," Rebecca suggested.

Christina thought about it. "Maybe."

"Or we could name her Whitebrook something or

other, like Whitebrook Lass," her father pointed out.

But Christina knew what she wanted to name the filly. "Her dam is Fleet Goddess and her sire is Jazzman," Christina said, looking down at the small foal. "So how about Jazz Goddess?"

"Yeah, that's a good idea," Rebecca said enthusiastically.

"I like it too," Christina's father said.

"Hurray, she did it!" Christina exclaimed, holding up the empty bottle. The foal instantly butted against Christina's legs, searching for more milk. "Oh, so now you're starving, huh?" Christina laughed. "Well, I guess I can rustle up another bottle for you somewhere. But how about a little rest for you first? I don't want you overdoing it."

The tiny foal looked up at Christina trustingly and blinked her wide brown eyes.

"You are such a sweetie," Christina murmured, rubbing the filly's head. Then the tiny foal settled down on the clean straw, collapsing with the sudden weariness of a baby. Christina sank down next to her, feeling pretty tired herself.

"Looks like bedtime," her dad said. "Just remember, in two hours you have to do this again."

Rebecca groaned and collapsed on her back in the straw.

"It's okay, Dad," Christina said. "Jazz Goddess is worth it."

3

"COME ON, GIRL, YOU CAN DO IT," CHRISTINA URGED Jazz.

Trustingly the filly hobbled across the large stall toward Christina.

"She's made progress in the last three weeks," Christina's father said, watching from over the stall door.

Christina nodded as the filly finally reached her and butted her small head against Christina's stomach. "Yeah. She's not growing as much as the other foals, but she is doing better. It's still kind of hard for her to walk, though."

"Well, it's great for her to get the exercise, so keep up the good work."

"Okay, Dad. Come on, Jazz. Follow me over here." Christina trotted around the stall until she was back at Fleet Goddess's side. The tall mare gently whoofed into Christina's hair, but her eyes were protectively watching her small foal. Jazz gamely but awkwardly walked over to Christina and her dam, and Fleet Goddess leaned over and licked the foal's head.

Because of Goddess's illness and the medicines used to treat her, her milk had dried up. But after a week of isolation and rest, Mr. Reese had let Jazz join her mother in a roomy stall. It had been touching to see their reunion and to realize they recognized each other at once, although they had spent so little time together.

The scene had brought tears to Christina's eyes. *What about you, Mom?* she silently asked her own mother. *Would you recognize me if you could see me?*

Now, after three weeks of round-the-clock bottle feeding, the foal had gained needed weight and had added inches to her height. Other foals were often out running around the paddock with their dams by the time they were a week or two old, but Jazz hadn't been outside yet—her legs were too weak.

The vet had cautioned Christina not to let the filly walk or run too much when she wasn't wearing her corrective boots, since that could cause her fetlocks to bend farther in. But when she *was* wearing her boots, she needed to run around as much as possible, to strengthen her muscles and encourage her legs to straighten out.

Sometimes it took all of Christina's persuasive

43

powers to keep the filly on her feet and moving around during these exercise sessions. Her deformed fetlocks made it difficult for her to walk for any distance, and the little boots only made things harder for her.

"Okay, Jazz, one more time around. Come on. Come on, sweetie. Once more for me," Christina coaxed. She walked back over to the other side of the stall, crouched down, and held open her arms. The filly looked at her tiredly, then nuzzled Fleet Goddess's side. "Come on, Jazz. Once more, please?"

Christina waited patiently, and then Fleet Goddess nudged the filly gently, almost pushing her toward Christina. It was as if she understood that her friend was trying to help her baby. Huffing out a little sigh, the filly trotted over to Christina.

"Yay! Good girl. Thanks, Jazz." Christina hugged the black foal, then scratched her behind both ears. "I know it's hard sometimes, girl. But you're brave and strong and I know you can do it." She hugged her again. These last three weeks, all her spare time had been taken up with feeding and exercising the foal, spending time with her and Fleet Goddess. Christina was exhausted. But it was all worth it, she knew, and once school let out for the summer, things would be easier.

One gorgeous Saturday in late May, Christina finally got the okay from Dr. Mendez to take Jazz outside. It was the moment she had been waiting for. Finally the filly's legs were strong enough to handle the sloping hills in Whitebrook's paddocks. At Christina's riding class that morning, she excitedly told Rebecca about it, and Rebecca had called her parents for permission to go to Whitebrook after class.

"I just can't believe Jazz is finally ready to go out into the paddock," Rebecca said as they headed toward the mares' barn. "The other foals have been out practically since they were born."

Christina led the way to Jazz's stall. "Yeah. I know Fleet Goddess will be glad to get outside too." Rather than risk the emotional trauma of even a temporary separation, Christina's father had decided to have Fleet Goddess stay indoors with the foal, instead of joining the other dams outside.

Inside Jazz's stall, Christina gently hooked a lead shank to the filly's small halter. At six weeks old, the foal was still quite a bit smaller and thinner than other foals her age. After only six weeks, though, the difference in Jazz's forelegs was obvious. Although she was still showing much too much inward curve in her ankles, it wasn't as bad as it had been when she was born. She still wore her corrective boots all the time, though, and probably would for several more months.

Rebecca hooked a lead shank to Goddess's halter, and the mare willingly followed her into the

45

aisle. But Jazz hesitated inside the safety of her stall, unwilling to venture into the unknown.

"Come on, sweetie," Christina urged her. "You're going outside today. Your mommy's going outside too, see? Don't you want to run and play in the grass?" Finally, unnerved at the sight of her mother disappearing down the aisle, Jazz timidly trotted after her, bleating a little cry.

"At least she's down to feeding every four hours. That must be a little easier," Rebecca said, pushing open the wide barn door while Goddess followed her docilely. The mare looked back to make sure her offspring was right behind her, then eagerly headed out into the sunlight.

"It is," Christina agreed.

At the open door of the barn the filly stopped dead, planting her small hooves firmly and refusing to budge. All she knew were the comforting sights, sounds, and smells of the barn where she was born. Now, confronted with the huge outdoors, filled with a million unknowns, the filly was terrified. And the sight of her mother heading confidently down the path to the small paddock didn't help.

"Jazz," Christina coaxed, "come on now. Look, Goddess is right there with Rebecca, and I'm right here beside you. We'll stay with you the whole way."

Rebecca paused for a moment with Goddess, giving the foal incentive to catch up to them.

"Whoa—first day outside, huh?" Kevin McLean

46

carefully leaned his small pitchfork against the wall of the barn. He ran his hand along the filly's straight, short back, then reached up and rubbed behind her pricked ears. "Hi, little girl," he said, smiling down at her.

Glancing at Christina, he said, "Maybe if we all go together she'll feel better." Stepping backward, facing the filly, he held out his hands. "Come on, girl. Listen to Uncle Kevin. You'll love it out here, I promise. Your mother's right there in front of you."

Snorting with laughter, Christina said, "Uncle Kevin?"

Kevin grinned. "Sure. Wait—I have an idea. Rebecca, you lead Goddess ahead slowly toward the little paddock. Chris, you come with me, ahead of the filly. When she sees you walking away, she'll want to follow you. You're her favorite person, after her dam."

"Her dam isn't exactly a person," Christina pointed out, but she did as Kevin said. Sure enough, when Jazz saw Christina moving out into the stable yard, she gave a tiny, panicked whinny, then took a hesitant step forward. The whole time Christina was coaxing her and urging her forward. Finally, in a burst of courage, the filly darted forward to stand trembling by Christina's side.

Laughing, Christina hugged the filly, then led her the rest of the way into a small fenced paddock where Rebecca and Goddess were already waiting.

Fearing that Jazz would be overwhelmed or picked on if she were put into the paddock with the larger foals and their dams, Christina had decided to let Goddess and Jazz stay by themselves awhile, with just Wonder for company. Goddess and Wonder were calmly munching sweet grass when Christina swung open the gate and walked in with Jazz. Goddess looked up and gave an encouraging whinny to her small foal, then resumed grazing.

At first the filly was too frightened to move and stood like a small black statue in the paddock next to Christina. Then her inquisitive nose started twitching as she took in all the delightful spring smells of Whitebrook. She blinked in the sunshine and bobbed her head. When Wonder casually strolled over and touched the filly gently, Jazz almost fell over.

"Give her twenty minutes," Rebecca predicted. "I bet she'll be trotting around like an old pro, boots or no boots."

"Her trotting is still pretty awkward, and she doesn't run well at all," Christina said, "but I bet being outside will help strengthen her legs a lot."

"Let's go see some of the other foals," Kevin suggested. "I think Jazz will be okay now."

Indeed, Jazz had wandered over to Goddess and was now so busy examining a pink clover flower that she didn't even notice their departure. Glancing back, Christina saw Jazz take one small experimental bite of fresh grass and chew thought-fully. Christina grinned.

Across the wide driveway, all the other spring foals were gamboling with their dams in the large front paddock.

"Wow. That one's gorgeous," Rebecca said admiringly, pointing at a tall, sleek colt.

"He's one of Pride's, out of Whitebrook Lass," Christina told her. "We named him True Gift. He was born in February."

"I've been watching him," Kevin said. "He's doing really well, growing fast. It would be great if he turned into something."

"It'd be great if *any* of them turned into something," Christina said.

"Dad said some of the two-year-olds are coming along well in training," Kevin added. "Like Wild Guess and White Lie."

"I can't wait until I can start helping with the training," Christina said, watching two of the foals chasing each other excitedly. "In the meantime I'm watching Dad and Mr. McLean as much as possible."

"Maybe they'll let you train Jazz when she's ready," Rebecca suggested.

Christina's eyes twinkled. "I already have it all planned. And you two can help! I'm going to be the first person on her back, you can be sure about that."

"Speaking of Jazz, look at her," Kevin said with a grin.

Across the driveway, Jazz was exploring her paddock as though she was determined to get every ounce of enjoyment out of the experience. Christina felt a small pang as she watched the filly awkwardly trying to gambol across the grass. Sighing, Christina wondered if Jazz's gaits would ever be improved enough for her to be ridden— much less race. Only time would tell.

"Chris! Eyes forward!" Tor Nelson called across the training oval several weeks later. "Keep him collected; don't let him run at the jump. Yes—good! That's the way!"

Whew, Christina thought, then focused her concentration squarely in front of her. She was in a new advanced-jumping class, which had four other students. Rebecca was one of them. With school out for the summer, Christina took classes almost every day, sometimes privately with just Tor, but more often with groups of other students.

Today there were five of them in the class. One at a time they jumped the course of fences set up around the ring while the others waited off to the side. Tor had set up a series of jumps that were more difficult than the ones they were used to in the intermediate class.

Now it was Christina's turn, and she was counting

silently, pacing Triumph against the jumps. *One, two, three, squeeze, and up,* Christina thought. At her signal, Triumph gathered his strong hindquarters and boosted them over a double combination. Instinctively Christina gave him rein and stretched herself smoothly over his neck, shifting the center of her balance as her pony jumped. Then they were landing lightly and cantering toward an oxer that was just ahead.

"Good, Chris, keep it up," Tor called.

One by one the class circled the course twice, then Tor clapped his hands for them to stop. "Very good, everyone," Tor told them. They had walked their ponies to the center of the ring to listen to his comments. "You're getting better at these exercises. Today, for the last twenty minutes of class, I want to review what we've learned so far about dressage."

Excitedly Christina turned to look at Rebecca, who gave her a thumbs-up. Both girls had been looking forward to expanding their repertoire, and dressage was an important part of advanced riding.

Patiently Tor went over some dressage terms that would lay the foundation for more-advanced work. "The most important thing is that both you and your mount appear relaxed, confident, and alert during a competition," he said. "In dressage your form is more important than ever. Dressage is a very old and elegant art form, and it requires very close communication between you and your mount. The two of you should move as one."

Then, taking his own horse, Top Hat, he swung up into the saddle and showed the class a few basic moves. Although the large white Thoroughbred was quite old, he was still beautiful, well muscled, and energetic. First Tor showed them sidestepping, where Top Hat stepped first to one side and then to the other. The class had seen this before and practiced it now with Tor watching. Then he led them through some leg yielding. To make their ponies go forward, they squeezed the ponies' sides with both calves. When the rider pressed with just one leg, the horse was to move in the opposite direction of where the pressure was applied.

As the class watched, Tor walked Top Hat first in a circle, then in a sort of hooked loop, then in a serpentine across the ring. Christina looked carefully, but she really couldn't see how Tor was getting Top Hat to perform those different moves. Tor sat so still on the horse's back that it looked as though Top Hat was doing everything by himself. But she knew it was a combination of almost hidden signals, like in the sidestepping and leg yielding, that allowed them to move like that. When they were done, the class clapped.

"We'll begin doing more-advanced dressage at next week's class," Tor told them. "In the meantime, practice your form. That's all for today."

Everyone dismounted and began to lead their

ponies back to the stabling area.

"Thanks, Tor," Christina and Rebecca said on their way out.

"Oh, Chris, and Rebecca—I wanted to talk to you," Tor said, taking Top Hat by the bridle. "There's an advanced-jumping show at the end of August at Briarsley, down in Danville." Danville was about an hour away from Lexington, and Briarsley was a famous hunt club there.

Christina nodded. "It's right before school starts. Last year we went to watch Mandy Jarvis compete."

"Right. Well, I'd like both of you to think about entering the advanced thirteen-and-under division."

"What?" Christina gasped. She and Rebecca turned to look at each other with wide eyes. "Tor, do you really think we're ready? We've only been taking advanced classes for two months."

Tor loosened the girth on Top Hat's saddle while the large white gelding waited patiently. Then, after slinging the saddle over a nearby fence rail, Tor turned to face the girls again. "By the time the show comes, you'll have had four months of advanced classes. And don't forget you've both been on horses since you could walk. Sammy and I think you've been doing terrifically in advanced jumping. In fact, I wanted to recommend that you both start focusing on some dressage and cross-country classes and stick to private lessons here for jumping."

Enthusiasm lit Christina's face. "Wow—advanced at Briarsley. That sounds great!" Then Christina gave a mock groan. "I've been waiting all year for summertime, and now that it's here, I just want it to be over so it'll be time for Briarsley!"

"Me too," Rebecca said with a laugh.

"Well, you guys don't have to register till the end of July. That should give you plenty of time to feel prepared."

"Okay." Christina nodded eagerly. "Thanks, Tor—this is really exciting. I can't wait to tell Dad about it!"

That afternoon Christina caught up to her father while he was in the mares' barn. Quickly she related what Tor had suggested and finished with a breathless "Isn't that great? It's what I've been waiting for—just another step on the ladder."

Mr. Reese looked down at his daughter with an amused look on his face. "What ladder is that?"

"You know," Christina began, "the ladder of competition. I'm making a real good start now, doing Briarsley advanced when I'm only ten. By the time I'm thirteen, I'll be in the seventeen-and-under advanced. Then, when I'm seventeen, I'll be at the National Horse Show, the Rolex Kentucky, and then . . ." She paused dramatically, her hazel eyes wide. "Then the Olympics!"

Her father leaned against a stall door, looking at her. "Chris, I had no idea you had all this planned. I mean, I know that you love jumping and are really good at it, but I didn't know that you've been planning so far ahead. Is that really what you see yourself doing? Why don't you just ride and enjoy it, and see where it takes you? You're only ten years old."

"Dad," Christina said patiently, "this is what I want to do. It's what I've always wanted to do."

"Qualifying for the Olympics takes a tremendous amount of work."

Christina shrugged. "I know. But it's what I want."

"But you're only ten. Maybe in a few years you'll feel differently," her dad began.

"Daaa-a-ad," Christina said, taking his arm. "When Mom was ten years old, do you think she knew what she wanted to do?"

"Well . . . I guess."

"Do you think she let the thought of hard work bother her?"

"Um . . . probably not," her father conceded.

"Do you think she had goals that she was working toward, even though she was only ten?" Christina persisted.

"Okay, okay." He laughed, holding up his hands. "I give up, give in, whatever. I see now that you're just as driven and determined as your mom was."

"And going to be just as great?" Christina asked saucily, cocking her head to one side.

"Yes," Mr. Reese said fondly, giving her a hug. "Going to be just as great. Now, let's go check on your filly, okay?"

In her stall, Jazz heard the sound of approaching feet and scampered to her door so she could peer out. At the sight of the small, elegantly shaped head, Christina smiled and quickened her pace.

"Hey, girl," she called. Jazz gave an excited whicker and pushed her head against the door. Goddess approached the stall door too and gently touched Christina's hair with her nose. Christina rubbed it.

"I'm surprised Jazz is even awake," her father said, reaching over the door to pat the filly's shoulder. "She played hard out in the paddock today."

Jazz went outdoors every day now. After her first day in the paddock three weeks earlier, she had shown only the slightest hesitation at the stable door, and now she eagerly followed Goddess outside. The fresh air and increased exercise seemed to have done her health good: her little legs seemed stronger and more muscular, and she had more energy and bounce. In just three weeks, her walking and trotting had smoothed out some, and yesterday Christina had seen her break into a clumsy canter.

Jazz was still just a baby, though, and usually

after a hard day of frolicking around Goddess and Wonder, she came back to her stall to nap exhaustedly.

"Did you have a good time, sweetie?" Christina asked, opening the door to let herself into the stall. Goddess calmly shifted her weight to give Christina room. "Oh, look at you—you're still covered with grass. Looks like you need a good grooming before dinner."

"Dr. Mendez says this filly is coming along better than he expected," her father said, looking over Jazz thoughtfully.

"Have you noticed how much better her ankles look?"

"Yeah, they do look better," her father acknowledged. "But they're still not up to par. As is, she couldn't be ridden."

"Dad, she's only two months old," Christina pointed out. "Give her a little time."

Mike Reese smiled ruefully and rubbed his hand across his chin. "Okay, sweetheart. I just want you to be aware of the facts, that's all. I know how hard you're working with the filly, and that's great. But in the end, you may never be able to ride her— even as a pleasure horse. Of course, since her problem isn't genetic, she could still be a valuable broodmare."

Just a broodmare? The thought rankled Christina. She knew the filly had far more potential than that.

Christina had to help her find that potential, that was all. Frowning, Christina said, "She's getting better all the time. I bet in six months you won't be able to tell she ever had a problem."

"I hope so, honey. Now I'll leave you to the grooming," Mr. Reese said as he shut the stall door. "Come to the house around six and help me with dinner, okay?"

"Okay," Christina agreed, getting out all her currying equipment.

Jazz, sensing that one of her favorite activities was coming up, was standing alertly in the middle of her stall. She loved being groomed, seeming to relish being the center of attention and perhaps knowing that she would look her best afterward.

As Christina started to brush the smooth, silky black coat, she talked quietly to the filly, communicating to her with words as well as with the tone of her voice.

"Don't worry, Jazz. We'll get all this grass out of your hair in no time. What did you do, fall asleep in a bank of clover?"

The filly whoofed softly, blowing warm, sweet breath over Christina's shoulder. Taking off the small leather boots that the filly still wore most of the time, Christina carefully examined the trim ankles underneath. They looked fine—still bent inward, but getting better all the time. Carefully she washed and dried Jazz's fetlocks, then washed and dried the leather boots. She set them aside and devoted herself to brushing out Jazz's mane and tail.

Although the filly had that odd white splotch over one ear and part of her face, she was still a beautiful example of a young Thoroughbred. Her coat was sleek and glossy, her eyes wide and intelligent. And even when she was bouncing excitedly around the paddock, she showed her breeding with her elegant lines and finely sculpted head. If it weren't for her weak fetlocks and small size, she would have been a filly for Whitebrook to be proud of.

"But I love you just the way you are, Jazz," Christina said quietly as she put away her grooming equipment. "I think you're beautiful, and brave, and perfect, right now. You've shown more heart in two months than a lot of horses show in their whole lives!" Putting her arms around the filly's neck, Christina kissed her, reveling in the warm scent of a clean and contented foal. "You just wait. We're going to show Dad how wrong he is. You're going to grow into something special—I feel it. And I'm going to be beside you every step of the way!"

4

"COME ON, I'LL RACE YOU TO THE CREST!" WITH A MIS-
chievous look over his shoulder, Kevin McLean
lightly touched his heels to the sides of his pony,
Lightning. They shot up the trail ahead of Christina
on Triumph and Rebecca on Maxie. Rebecca's father
had vanned the two ponies over from Tor's that
morning so they could have a group ride over
the Whitebrook trails.

"Are we going to let him get away with that?"
Christina demanded.

"No!" Rebecca cried, giving Maxie the signal to
tear off after Kevin.

Christina smiled determinedly, then pulled up
her stirrups, hunched over Triumph's withers, and
clucked her tongue. "Go, boy!" she yelled, and the
pony didn't have to be urged further. Instantly he
switched gears from an easy trot to a fast-paced

gallop, his powerful hind legs churning up the packed dirt of the trail.

In her backpack Christina had a picnic lunch, as well as a towel. On this hot, mid-July day, she wore her bathing suit under her clothes.

Slowly the three ponies made their way down a steeper winding trail to the small, stream-fed pond that served as a swimming pool in the summer. Once there, the ponies waded into the shallow pond, bent their heads, and drank their fill of the cool, fresh water. Then Rebecca, Kevin, and Christina tied their mounts beneath the shady trees on the bank. There they peacefully munched on grass and lazily switched away flies with their tails.

"Swim first, then lunch?" Rebecca asked, and the other two nodded.

The next hour was filled with swimming, splashing contests, dunking, and floating contentedly in the pond. Then, ravenous, Christina climbed out of the water and flopped onto her towel to open her lunch bag. Rebecca and Kevin followed, spreading their own towels on the warm, grassy bank. Soon they were all digging into their picnic lunches, enjoying the feeling of the summer sun drying their skin and hair.

"Have you decided about Briarsley?" Rebecca asked, taking a sip of her soda.

Christina nodded. "I'm going to do it. I'll tell Tor tomorrow at class so he can send in the application."

Grinning, Rebecca admitted, "I want to do it too. Even if I don't win a ribbon, it'll be good experience."

"I'm sure Ross Townsend will be competing there," Christina added with a frown.

Ross Townsend was the same age as Christina and had always been one of her biggest rivals on the jumping circuit. But their rivalry went back even further than that. Townsend Acres, the farm Ross's grandfather owned, was in constant competition with Christina's father's farm. It was a long-standing rivalry that had started before Christina was born. Christina's mother had co-owned a number of horses with Ross's grandfather, so Christina and her father visited Townsend Acres often to check on the horses that Mr. Reese now co-owned. Whenever Christina bumped into Ross, he always had something nasty to say.

"You guys let Ross get to you too much. Why don't you just ignore him? Anyway, I'll never figure out why any of you, including Ross, like jumping so much," Kevin said, lying on his back to soak up the sun. "Flat racing is so much more exciting. I can't wait till I can start helping Dad train horses."

"Jumping is definitely better than flat racing," Rebecca said, crumpling up her sandwich wrapper. "With flat racing, you just do the same thing again and again. The horse only has to go faster— it doesn't have to think that much. And the rider just has to worry about staying on. With jumping, both the rider and the horse really have to pay attention and make decisions as they go. It's *much* more exciting."

Kevin sat bolt upright, his eyes wide. "You can't believe that!" he sputtered. "Flat racing is so much more demanding. You have to run against all sorts of other horses. You have to pay attention to what everyone around you is doing. And because you're moving so fast, you have to make split-second decisions all the time!" His red hair stuck straight up from swimming, and his green eyes were round with indignation. "Christina—tell her she's wrong," he demanded. "After all, your mom was one of the best jockeys around. Obviously she thought flat racing was the best."

Grinning, Christina held up her hands for peace. "Don't put me in the middle! I totally love jumping, but flat racing is exciting too. They're two different things. You can't really compare them. And I think what was most important to my mom was the animals themselves, really getting to know the horses, helping them to be their best no matter what."

"That makes sense. Let's call a truce," Rebecca said, smiling at Kevin. "Here—I'll even split my brownie with you."

"Oh, okay," Kevin grumbled, taking the brownie. "But still I—" He broke off with a gasp when both girls threw their wadded-up trash at him.

"Truce, Kevin, remember?" Christina laughed.

The following week Whitebrook had a horse running in a maiden allowance race at Churchill Downs, in Louisville. It was just a small race for two-year-olds, but Mike and Ian McLean, as co-owner and cotrainer of the colt, wanted Runaway to get his feet wet. Mr. Wonderful, a son of Ashleigh's Wonder, had sired Runaway, and Whitebrook Lass was his dam. He had been training very well all summer and looked promising.

Two days before the race, Christina and her father vanned Runaway over to the Churchill Downs track, about sixty miles from their home in Lexington. Arriving early would give Runaway plenty of time to get used to his new surroundings.

"How's the boy this morning?" Ian McLean asked the next day as he and Kevin walked up to Runaway's stall on the backside of the Downs.

"Good," Mr. Reese said. "The ride over doesn't seem to have bothered him. He ate a good breakfast this morning."

"Who's going to be riding him tomorrow?" Christina asked.

"Fidel Varela," her father answered, naming one of Whitebrook's regular jockeys, a young Hispanic rider.

"Come on, Chris," Kevin said. "Let's walk

around and look at the other horses. Okay, Dad?"

Ian McLean smiled down at his son. "Yeah. Come back here when you're done. We're just going to look Runaway over, make sure he's a hundred percent, and then we'll all go have lunch somewhere."

"Okay," Kevin agreed.

Slowly the two friends walked down the line of stalls that ran behind the racetrack at Churchill Downs. They knew quite a few of the owners or trainers, at least by sight, and smiled hello to them.

"Wow, he's a beauty, huh?" Kevin said softly, pointing to a large bay Thoroughbred. "And look at that one. He's gorgeous."

Christina smiled. Kevin was as horse-crazy as she was, and he almost always found something good to say about a horse.

"I thought that was you," a voice called from behind them.

Christina cringed. She knew that voice all too well. It was Ross Townsend. "Hello, Ross," she said coolly, barely giving him a glance.

"I see you've got one of Mr. Wonderful's two-year-olds entered in a maiden allowance tomorrow," Ross said, ignoring Christina's cold tone.

"Yes, we do. Runaway."

"Well, you haven't had a decent runner in a while. Maybe this one will get lucky."

Christina gritted her teeth and bit back the cutting

response she wanted to make. Ross could never find anything nice to say.

"I hear you're competing at Briarsley next month," he went on.

"I am. So?"

"Just that I heard you're going to compete in advanced. So am I. Which means you're going to lose, but I guess you're used to that." Ross gave her a condescending smile.

"Ross, why don't you make like an egg and beat it?" Kevin said angrily.

"Oh, that's original, McLean. Good one. Why don't you tell me to take a long walk off a short pier?"

"Sounds like a good idea to me," Christina shot back.

Ross laughed. "Well, see you later, losers." He turned and sauntered away, leaving Christina with smoke coming out of her ears.

"I can't stand him," Christina muttered as she and Kevin made their way back to Whitebrook's assigned stabling.

"He's a jerk, all right," Kevin agreed.

Fuming silently all the way back to Runaway's stall, Christina didn't mention her private fear: what if Ross was right, and she did badly at Briarsley? She and Ross had competed before, during both novice and intermediate shows. Ross had always beaten her. And he had always gloated obnoxiously about it.

Well, I'll just have to do better than ever, Christina told herself. *I know I can do well on Triumph. I'm going to show Ross Townsend once and for all. My mom always came out on top against the Townsends, and so will I.*

Runaway's race was second on the card the following afternoon. Christina and Kevin went to the saddling paddock first, to wish the big colt luck, and then made their way to Whitebrook's reserved seats in the owners' section of the grandstand.

"This is exciting," Christina said. "I can't believe this is the first race I've been to all summer and one of our horses is running!" Christina settled back in her seat and pulled a pair of binoculars out of her knapsack. Quickly she scanned the track. The race was only seven furlongs. The starting gate was already in place at the head of the backstretch.

"I know," Kevin said eagerly. "I really like Runaway. I want him to win big. My dad thinks he could be our next graded-stakes winner."

Christina grinned at her friend. "You're really planning ahead, aren't you?" In her heart, Christina shared Kevin's hopes. Whitebrook was due for a big, graded-stakes winner—a star. Her father and Mr. McLean had several decent allowance horses running and winning enough to pay the bills, but none that had that extra quality and spark of talent that would enable them to compete against the best—like Wonder had and Fleet Goddess, Jazzman and Wonder's Pride.

Soon the horses and their jockeys came out onto the dirt track, accompanied by escort ponies and riders. Christina and Kevin cheered as they saw Runaway with Fidel Varela on his back in the blue-and-white silks of Whitebrook. As the horses finished their warm-up lap, Mr. Reese and Ian McLean joined Christina and Kevin in the grandstands.

Through her binoculars, Christina could see Runaway being loaded into the number-four position.

"Should be okay for the colt," her father murmured, and Mr. McLean nodded.

Then the announcer cried, "And they're off!" The gates broke open and seven gleaming two-year-old Thoroughbreds leaped out onto the dirt simultaneously.

"Go, Runaway!" Christina yelled as she watched the horses thunder away from the gate and onto the backstretch. The number-two horse, Stairway to Heaven, got an early lead, but Runaway and another colt, Prince Henry, were neck and neck for second place. From hearing hours of discussion by her father and Ian McLean, Christina knew that Runaway tended to get out in the front of any pace horses and just stay there. But Stairway to Heaven didn't look like he was ready to give up his early lead, and Christina's brow creased with worry.

Although Christina loved the challenge of show-jumping, she found flat racing exciting to watch, especially when a Whitebrook horse was running. The combined energy of the crowd in the grandstands, the smell of horses and hay, the warmth of the July sun, all added up to a thrilling experience. She knew this was her mother's world—her mom had lived for racing and had been deeply involved with every aspect of it. Christina beamed with pride whenever anyone mentioned her mother's legendary successes on the track. *Someday I'm going to be that successful*, Christina thought. *Just like my mom. Only, I'm going to do it in jumping.* Christina had been attending races practically her whole life, since her father or Townsend Acres usually had at least one horse on the field at most of the major races. But she never got tired of seeing Thoroughbreds trying their hardest, pushing to get ahead, racing the wind in an attempt to be number one. It was a feeling like nothing else.

"Come on, Runaway, come on, boy!" she yelled as the horses swept around the far turn. They were on the homestretch now—in moments they would pour across the finish line. Stairway to Heaven had the lead. Runaway was a length behind in second, and Prince Henry had dropped back into fourth, behind Another Cup.

Kevin joined her in yelling, "Come on, Runaway!"

Christina sat glued to the edge of her seat as Runaway, in a last-second burst of speed, pulled up alongside Stairway to Heaven. As the horses roared across the finish line, it was impossible to see who had actually won.

"And it's a photo finish, ladies and gentlemen!" the announcer cried. "Stairway to Heaven and Runaway in what looks to be a dead heat!"

"I hope Runaway got it!" Christina cried, looking at her father. "How did it look to you?"

"It looked absolutely nose to nose," her dad told her. "Either way, the colt made an impressive showing today. We can definitely start thinking about aiming him toward some bigger races at the end of summer or early fall." A pleased and excited smile lit his face.

It seemed to take forever for the judges to review the video, Christina thought. She bounced impatiently in her seat. *If only Mom could be here.* She swallowed hard as she let herself dwell on what that would be like: she, her mom, and her dad, all sitting together in the owners' box. Her mother would be excited, jumping up and down . . . her dad would be so happy and proud. Maybe her mother would even still be riding Whitebrook's horses. Christina thought of the photo on the mantel of her mom's trim figure in the blue-and-white silks of their farm. If her mother were riding Runaway, it would be a double victory if they won. Smiling wistfully,

Christina enjoyed her daydream for a few moments more. It would have been so wonderful, she thought, to have that. If only her mother were still alive, it would all be so perfect.

She snapped out of her daydream when the speakers erupted with static, then the announcer's voice came blaring out: "And the winner is Stairway to Heaven, by a *hair*! Runaway a very, very close second. Another Cup in third. A very close race, ladies and gentlemen, a very close race indeed."

As disappointed as the group from Whitebrook was, it had been so close that they could still be proud of Runaway's performance. Christina followed her father as he made his way down to the winner's circle to congratulate Stairway's owners and then to see about Runaway.

Later, as she drooped sleepily against her father's shoulder in the cab of the truck heading back to Whitebrook, she heard him say, "After all, what matters is that he put his heart into it. He ran his best, and that's all we can ask for. Don't forget that, Chris. Your mom would have wanted you to know that."

"I do," Christina mumbled, not opening her eyes. *But that won't be good enough when I go against Ross Townsend* was the last thought she had before falling asleep.

5

"I CAN'T BELIEVE WE'RE AT BRIARSLEY!" ALTHOUGH SHE
had come last year to watch Mandy Jarvis compete,
now that she was here to compete herself, it looked
completely different. Christina gazed around the
bustling showgrounds with excitement. The sun
had been up all of fifteen minutes, but everywhere
she looked, horses were being walked or groomed
or worked on longe lines. Two huge fields were
filled with horse vans and pickup trucks, even
some motor homes from out of state. Competitors
from all over the East Coast had set up their folding
chairs near their vans and were now mingling in
groups. Christina had already talked to quite a few
kids whom she knew from the riding circuit.
Beyond the mass of vans were the warm-up and
show-jumping rings, the concession stands, and the
officials' tent.

"I can't believe it either," Rebecca said, nervously smoothing her short, curly brown hair.

Christina took a deep breath. The August day was sweltering, and the air was stifling and heavy, even though it was barely five thirty in the morning. Christina hoped the heat wouldn't affect Triumph's performance. They had left Whitebrook at four o'clock that morning to make the one-hour drive to Danville, where Briarsley took place.

But Christina didn't have time to gawk. She and Rebecca had work to do. Fortunately, Kevin had offered to come along and act as groom, and they had gratefully accepted. First the horses had to be unloaded from the van. Then, with Kevin's help, the girls would carefully groom their mounts, braid Maxie and Triumph's manes and tails, put on fresh hoof oil, and brush their sleek coats until they gleamed. After they finished grooming the ponies, they would take turns giving them a short work on a longe line in an open field near the ring. That would keep Triumph and Maxie on their toes.

"How's it going, girls?" Christina's father asked them an hour later.

"Okay, Dad," Christina said bravely, though inside she was feeling anything but. *Just relax—you've jumped similar courses at home and at class. You'll do fine. Triumph will do his best.*

"Here," her father said, handing them each a

muffin and a small container of juice. "Try to get this in you before you start."

Smiling at her dad, Christina took the muffin. He knew that she had been too nervous to eat earlier. She was always tense before a competition; partly because she wanted to do well and jump her best, and partly because in some way, she felt she had to live up to her mother's image. After all, Ashleigh had won the Kentucky Derby when she was only sixteen years old. Christina was very proud of her mother's accomplishments, and she wanted to show that she was her mother's daughter.

"We better go check in and get our numbers," she told Rebecca. The advanced thirteen-and-under class was jumping at ten o'clock. A list of who was competing and in what classes would probably be posted by now. Usually Christina liked jumping about fifth in the list. That way, she had enough time to watch the other riders, and it helped her plan her strategy.

Christina and Rebecca signed in with the officials and collected their numbers. "Ugh," Christina groaned when she saw that she was jumping third. "I was hoping to have more time to study the course. With only two people in front of me, it'll be hard to see exactly where the trouble spots are."

"Well, I lucked out," Rebecca said. "I'm eighth. And look who comes right before me."

"Ross Townsend." Christina frowned. "So he gets to watch me first."

"Try not to think about it," Rebecca pleaded. "You know you're ready for this—more ready than I am. Now let's go find Tor, then we'll change into our habits." The girls had worn jeans and T-shirts to groom the horses and practice. Before the actual competition they would change into riding breeches, sleeveless blouses, and riding jackets. They weren't looking forward to having to put on jackets on such a hot, muggy day.

Several hours later, their division was called to walk the course. The jumps were changed for each of the different classes competing that day. Earlier the novice pony divisions had jumped. Later would come the junior and adult divisions. Christina and Rebecca headed toward the gate, where Tor was waiting for them.

The course had been designed by a famous ex–show-jumper who had competed in the Olympics, and it looked very difficult. Although Christina and Triumph had jumped over these types of obstacles before, the course was laid out with several very tight turns. It would take all her concentration to judge Triumph's strides and pace him correctly.

It was by far the most difficult course Christina had ever attempted, and suddenly she felt as though she had bitten off more than she could chew. At only ten years old, she and Rebecca were the youngest jumpers competing in their division. The rest of the field, except of course for Ross Townsend, were all twelve- or thirteen-years-old. There was one eleven-year-old. *Ross is your age and he's doing it*, Christina told herself staunchly. *Anything he can do, you can do better.* Except that hadn't been the case in the past.

When Christina and Rebecca had finished walking the course, Tor talked to them and gave them his advice. There were eight jumps in all, including two tight turns and one medium-tight turn.

"That first parallel and the brush should be no problem," Tor said. "Rebecca, remember to keep Maxie very collected on this course. You know she has a tendency to lengthen her stride between jumps."

Rebecca nodded.

"Then there's the triangle, which you'll jump over at its smallest point, as though it were a single jump. It looks scary, but it's really no bigger or wider than other jumps you've done."

Tor talked them through the rest of the course: the first tight turn from a crossbar into an oxer, then a straight stretch over two easy verticals, another tight turn over the wide part of the triangle, where they would have to jump in and out very quickly, and the last turn over a brush-water combination. It was true that both girls had done all of these jumps before, but never with such difficult turns and under such pressure.

Smiling at them reassuringly, Tor said, "I know you two can do it. Just concentrate, listen to what your pony is telling you, and move as one. Go get your horses and try to relax, okay? I'll wait here for you."

Wordlessly, Christina and Rebecca nodded, then headed back to the van area where Kevin and Christina's dad were waiting. Quickly the two girls changed into their riding clothes inside Triumph's stall with the door closed. Christina's throat was dry, and her hands felt clammy.

"Honey, are you all right?" her father said, seeing Christina's white face when she came out. She nodded and found a hay bale to sit on. She wanted to go back into Triumph's stall and hug him for reassurance, but she knew that he would pick up on her fear and nervousness, and it would make him nervous too.

"I'm okay. It's a tough course," she admitted.

Kevin came over to hand her a soda. "You'll ace it," he predicted firmly.

Christina smiled up at him. "Thanks, pal."

"Honey, I see someone I want to go talk to. Will you be okay on your own for a few minutes?" her dad asked.

"Sure, Dad."

"So you didn't chicken out, huh? I'm shocked."

The snide tones of Ross Townsend startled Christina. Instantly she was on guard, already feeling a bubble of anger rising in her throat. Ross Townsend was dressed in an expensive riding habit. Christina had heard he had his clothes made especially for him by a tailor in London.

Before Christina could reply, Mr. and Mrs. Townsend, Ross's parents, arrived. Lavinia Townsend looked cool and immaculate in a violet-colored linen dress, and Brad looked as though he had stepped from the pages of *Horse & Rider* magazine.

"Oh, hello, Christina," Lavinia said. "I didn't know you were riding today. You're entered in the intermediate class?"

"I'm in advanced," Christina said. The Townsends were never actually mean or rude to her, but somehow Ross's parents managed to make her feel about two inches tall whenever she saw them.

"Oh, goodness." Lavinia gave a cool smile. "Congratulations. You and Ross will be riding against each other."

"I know." Christina looked away, feeling uncomfortable.

"I'm getting a new horse on my next birthday," Ross suddenly put in. "Then I'll win more than ever. Right, Mom?"

Lavinia Townsend smiled indulgently at her son. "That's right, dear. We're going to get you the best horse money can buy. Now, we better get to the ring. The first rider is about to go off. Bye, Christina."

Mrs. Townsend looked at Rebecca as though trying to figure out if she knew her or not. Then, with a slight shrug, she walked away, followed by her husband and son.

"I can't believe she doesn't know who I am. I've only met her a million times, either at your place or at Townsend Acres when I've gone over with you and your dad," Rebecca said in disgust. She put on her hard hat and fastened the chin strap firmly.

"But, Rebecca, you're one of the little people," Kevin teased her. "You're not important enough to be remembered."

Groaning, Christina fastened her own hard hat. "Those people are so awful," she grumbled. "It must be genetic. I just wish Ross wasn't jumping today."

"You'll do great," Kevin argued, unclipping Triumph and leading him from the stall. He gave Christina a leg into the saddle, and then Mr. Reese came back to walk with them and wait beside the show ring with the other competitors in the advanced thirteen-and-under class. "I bet you beat him hands down."

But Christina was too far gone for assurances. Butterflies were waging war in her stomach. She knew she had to get a grip on herself—soon her nervousness would translate to Triumph, and he would act up. If only she could concentrate on the course and forget about Ross Townsend!

She and Triumph waited beside Rebecca and Maxie and all the other riders and their mounts: ten jumpers in all. Then, at the tinkling of the judges' bell, the first rider trotted into the ring.

Christina recognized the first competitor, Catherine Gomila. She had been in the advanced thirteen-and-under class for more than a year and was very good. Catherine paused to salute the judges, then began circling her pony in a canter to approach the first jump.

Christina watched intently, noting where she would have to gather Triumph in, where she could let him out a little to gather speed. The crowd murmured as Catherine ticked the second jump, a rail, and then ticked again going over the second jump in the combination. This time the rail wobbled and fell.

Next to Christina, Rebecca muttered, "Course must be tougher than it looks. And that's saying something."

A cold trickle of sweat ran down Christina's back. If an experienced advanced rider like Catherine was having trouble, how would she and Triumph fare? But she couldn't allow herself to think of the negatives or she'd really be a basket case.

Catherine finished the course with a total of three knockdowns, unusually many for her. She looked distressed and embarrassed as she rode her pony off the course, and Christina felt sympathy for her.

Then it was the next rider's turn, a twelve-year-old boy named Mark Spencer. Biting her lip, Christina studied Mark and his mount as they circled toward the first jump. She and Triumph would be the next to compete. Again, she felt her stomach flutter.

Mark Spencer did better than Catherine, but it was obvious he was unhappy about his performance. His time had also been a little slow, but in this particular division, the riders weren't competing against the clock.

As Mark rode out, Christina took a deep breath, straightened her shoulders, and trotted Triumph into the ring. She wondered if her mother had ever been this nervous before a race. Then, suddenly, she heard a calming voice calling to her. "Don't worry, Christina," the voice said. "Trust in yourself, and trust in Triumph. You'll be fine, you'll be fine. I love you, Christina. I know that you'll make me proud."

Christina and Triumph were in the ring. She had no time to wonder about the mysterious voice. Forcing herself to concentrate, she saluted the judges with a nod, then heeled Triumph into a collected canter. Surprisingly, though, as she headed Triumph toward the first jump, a parallel, she felt a wave of calm float over her. Suddenly nothing else existed but these jumps, the wind on her face, the sun on her skin, the smell of the dirt, and the feel of her powerful pony beneath her. They cleared the parallel easily, as though they had flown over it.

Keeping Triumph collected, Christina made a small turn and headed him toward the brush. It was several inches higher than the brushes she was used to, but she counted strides mentally, thinking, *One, two, three, squeeze,* and they were up and over. Straight ahead was the triangle, and again they went over clean. Now Christina was smiling, feeling calm and relaxed and in total control. This was what she loved, what she was good at. If she just put her heart and soul into it, Triumph would too, and they would come out on top. She knew that. It was what the voice had been telling her.

After the triangle there was a crossbar, and immediately after they landed from that, Christina turned Triumph in a very tight half-circle. With only two short strides before the next jump, an oxer, Christina held her breath. Then she squeezed with her legs and automatically gave Triumph rein. She felt the pony gather his hindquarters and push off. Christina stretched over his withers and neck, helping him keep his center of gravity low. They soared over the oxer, landed smoothly, and took four long strides toward a double vertical jump. She collected Triumph as they approached and squeezed hard with her legs.

And they were over! Beneath her Triumph felt as though he had wings, and the sunlight glinted off his shiny bay coat. Two strides after the double vertical, there was another very tight turn as she headed back to jump in and out over the wide part of the triangle.

"Come on, Triumph," she muttered between clenched teeth. So far they had jumped cleanly, but these in-and-outs were notoriously difficult. *One, two, squeeze, and IN, bounce once, squeeze, and UP and OUT* . . . Triumph landed lightly on the outside, as though the substantial obstacles had been mere cavalletti that he had pranced over. Then there was one more turn and the last jump: a wide water jump preceded by a high brush.

Triumph would need to make a long, powerful jump to clear both obstacles. Christina squeezed hard on Triumph's sides, and the pony pushed with his powerful hindquarters, launching them into the air. Christina was oblivious to the crowds, to the judges, to everything except the sheer joy of flying through the bright sunlight.

They cleared it! Triumph's back hooves pounded down a good six inches past the water, and beaming, Christina circled him, slowing him to a trot as they headed back to the gate. The sound of applause and cheering reached her ears, and she searched the bleachers for her father and Kevin. Her dad was on his feet, punching his fist in the air. Kevin put two fingers in his mouth and whistled. Christina gave her father a thumbs-up, which he returned. Then she was out of the show ring.

Rebecca beamed at Christina. "You did great!" she called. "Perfect! I couldn't see one thing wrong! I just hope I can do as well."

Now that it was over, Christina felt full of joy and relief. In a way, it didn't matter how well she had done—she had given it her all, and so had Triumph, and she knew she would be happy with that. But the judges were reading her score.

"Christina Reese, no faults. A perfect round," the judge announced, and Christina almost laughed out loud. Quickly dismounting, she found herself swept into a hug by Tor, who lifted her in the air and swung her around. She threw her own arms around Triumph and gave him a huge hug. Kissing his nose, his cheek, and his forehead, she cried, "Thank you, Triumph! We did great—you and me together!" Then she hugged Tor again.

"Congratulations, Chris," Tor said. "I'm really proud of you. I know your dad is, too. Walk Triumph around while the rest of the division jumps. You two will definitely be going back into the ring for a ribbon."

"Yeah. Thanks, Tor."

She pulled up the stirrups and walked Triumph on the grass near the show ring until it was Ross's turn to compete. Then she led Triumph closer to the ring to watch.

Ross looked tense but concentrated, and Christina noted reluctantly that his seat in the saddle was almost perfect. *No wonder,* she thought. *He's been having private lessons practically his whole life. And his pony is one of the best in the country.* But she pushed those thoughts out of her head and leaned against Triumph lovingly.

Ross and his pony, Royal Dream, easily cleared the first parallel jump and the brush. Christina held her breath as they went over the narrow end of the triangle. She knew how intimidating it looked when you were right on top of it. Then there was the crossbar, and he cleared that, too. The oxer was next, then the double vertical. So far they had jumped clean. But at the next obstacle, the in-and-out over the large part of the triangle, Christina frowned. Ross hadn't given Royal Dream enough leg, and although they cleared the first fence, they ticked the second one on the way out. The pole tottered, then fell.

Then Ross turned and headed toward the brush–water jump, and here he had clearly recognized his mistake, because he urged Royal Dream hard, and they sailed over it.

"Ross Townsend, four faults," the judge announced. Ross looked angry and disappointed when he rode out of the ring, and instantly he dismounted.

His parents came up to him, but he brushed by them and stalked off, handing his pony's reins to his father. Brad Townsend hastily thrust Royal Dream's bridle into the hands of a waiting groom, then left to follow his son.

With a final frown at Christina, Lavinia followed them.

Christina hardly had time to think about Ross's spoilsport behavior or to feel sorry for Royal Dream, who was being treated unfeelingly, because it was time for Rebecca's round.

"You'll do great, I know it," Christina said as soon as Rebecca's name was called. "I'll be sending you good vibes the whole way."

Rebecca gave a wobbly smile. "Thanks—I'll need them." Then she headed Maxie into the show ring.

Like Christina, Rebecca had an unusually good round, but came in with four faults.

"Still," she said breathlessly when the judges announced her score, "it's much better than I thought I'd do! I'm just glad it's over."

"Me too," Christina said with heartfelt emotion.

Christina watched tensely as the last two competitors jumped. She was sure at least one other rider would go clean, and up until the last fence, she was afraid the last rider would do it. But the rider didn't give enough leg going over the water and his mount's rear hooves landed inside the tape.

Christina stood in stunned silence for a moment. Then Rebecca turned to give her a hug. "You won it! You get the blue!"

Tor hurried up to her, followed by Mr. Reese and Kevin. Tor was beaming as he held Triumph so Christina could remount and ride into the ring with the other four top finishers.

"You did it, pumpkin," her father called to her with a beaming smile.

"I had help," she whispered back. Although Triumph had certainly given one hundred percent, Christina knew that it had been the mysterious voice that had helped her pull through.

Christina proudly rode Triumph into the ring, and the judge fastened the blue ribbon onto his halter. Then he handed Christina a small gold trophy of a horse and rider and shook her hand.

Ross, scowling and looking as if he wished Christina would just disappear, was second. A thirteen-year-old was in third place, and a twelve-year-old was in fourth.

Although Christina was drooping with exhaustion from the tension of the day, when she got back to Whitebrook, she stopped to check on Jazz before she turned in.

"Hey, little girl," she crooned, and was rewarded by the small filly's immediately scampering to the stall door to see her.

Now five months old, Jazz was continuing to fill out and grow. Her fetlocks were getting better all the time, and Dr. Mendez thought she would have to wear her little corrective boots only another couple months or so.

Wearily Christina kissed the filly's head and stroked her neck. "Maybe someday you and I can jump together, Jazz," she whispered. "That is, if you don't turn into a fabulous racehorse that Dad would want!" With a final smile and a kiss, Christina headed out into the balmy August night.

Christina looked up to the stars that were almost obscured by a billowy cloud. "I'm on the ladder, Mom," she whispered. "I'm going to make you proud of me—and I'm going to make me proud of me, too." Smiling, Christina headed for the welcoming glow of the farmhouse. Suddenly she stopped in her tracks. "And thanks for your help today, Mom. You said all the right things." Then she turned and went inside.

Part Two

6

"OKAY, JAZZ, GO! LET'S GO, GIRL!" CHRISTINA TAPPED her heels against the Thoroughbred's sleek sides, and obediently the filly leaped ahead. Hunching low over Jazz Goddess's withers, Christina urged the filly onward. As they flew past the quarter-mile pole, she kneaded her hands along Jazz's neck, clucking with her tongue and asking Jazz to switch into a higher gear. Gamely the three-year-old put in another burst of speed, but Christina had exercise-ridden enough of her father's horses to know that Jazz was performing adequately, not fantastically. As they passed the last marker pole, she stood in the saddle, then slowed Jazz to a canter. "Whoa, girl, whoa. Good girl, Jazz. Let's head back." Inside, Christina felt a prickle of frustration that she was determined not to show the filly. It wasn't Jazz's fault she hadn't suddenly turned into a spectacular flat racer by the time she was three. Christina didn't know what the problem was.

At the gap to the training oval Mike Reese waited, stopwatch in hand. "How'd she feel?" he asked.

Christina shook her head and unfastened her hard hat strap before dismounting. Even though it was still only April, she had worked up a sweat by riding so hard. Now she shook out her short blond hair and ruffled it with her fingers. "Like she always does," she told her father. "She's willing, and she has great form, but she just doesn't seem to need to win."

Christina's father frowned. "Her fetlocks delayed her initial training, because we wanted to make sure she was a hundred percent fit. Then she was too gangly as a two-year-old to do much good, but she's grown into herself now." He held the filly's bridle and stroked a hand along the gleaming black neck. "She's a beautiful animal. But she's just not showing that extra spark."

Christina sighed. She and her father had had this discussion several times before. The little foal who had been born so handicapped had grown into a tall, beautiful, powerful Thoroughbred, with excellent conformation, an elegant head, and alert, intelligent eyes. Everything about her said she should be a star on the racetrack. But although Christina kept wishing and praying for it to happen, it just hadn't. Not yet.

Now Mr. Reese was becoming frustrated. It was very expensive to keep a Thoroughbred in training, and he had several other horses he needed to devote his time and resources to. Christina knew he would have to make a decision soon, and she was afraid of what that decision might be.

As Christina walked Jazz Goddess up and down the stable yard, cooling her out, she reflected on the changes that had occurred in the last three years. At thirteen Christina was tall for her age and slender. Her blond hair was still cut short, but the older she got, the more she resembled pictures of her mother.

She had long since outgrown her beloved pony, Triumph, and two years before had sold him to a younger girl in one of Tor's classes. Christina knew that Triumph was in good hands, but she still missed him terribly.

Since then, Christina and her friend Rebecca Morrison both had continued to take jumping and dressage classes from Tor and Samantha at the Nelsons' stable. And Christina's father had set up a cross-country course on the back trails of White-brook. There the two girls spent many hours practicing their jumping. Rebecca had a new mount, Marbella, a nice warmblood horse who was a good size for her and nimble on the field. Christina, though, hadn't found anyone to replace Triumph. Over the past two years she had tried one horse after another, using some of her father's retired racers and some of Samantha and Tor's stable horses, but she just hadn't found the perfect match yet. For three-day eventing, which she was focusing on, a mount had to be agile, powerful, full of stamina and heart, and also very intelligent. Unfortunately, a horse like that usually cost a great deal. Although she was reluctant to do it, Christina had lately been considering dipping into the trust money her mother had left her when she died. But she wasn't sure her father would agree to it.

If only I could have Jazz, Christina thought. Not for the first time she wondered if Jazz might have talent as a jumper, and if she would be any better at three-day eventing than she was at flat racing. Looking at the filly next to her, Christina was overwhelmed with love for Jazz. They had been through thick and thin—there was an unshakable bond between them unlike anything Christina had ever felt for a horse. Sometimes Christina was sure Jazz knew exactly what she was thinking and vice versa. One look at Jazz's head, her expressive face, her large, liquid brown eyes, and Christina knew what the filly was feeling. With Jazz continuing to be a disappointment in her flat training, Christina was thinking more and more of asking her father for a chance to retrain Jazz as a jumper. But she hadn't been able to get up the nerve yet.

"Okay, girl. Let's get you back in your stall and give you some breakfast." Jazz bobbed her sleek black head in agreement, and they headed toward the large open door of the training barn. "Hey. How'd her workout go?" Kevin asked. He had True Gift in crossties in the middle aisle and was grooming the promising Thoroughbred. True Gift had been born the same spring as Jazz, and now as a three-year-old he was the shining star of Whitebrook. The son of Wonder's Pride and Whitebrook Lass, he had fulfilled everyone's dreams and hopes during his training and had already proven himself by winning two big stakes races for three-year-olds. In a little more than a week True Gift was going to run in a Kentucky Derby prep race, the Bluegrass, at Keeneland in Lexington.

"It was okay," Christina said, trying not to let her disappointment show. After she had untacked Jazz Goddess, groomed her quickly, and gotten her settled in her stall with a full hay net, she came to sit beside Kevin on a bale of hay while he worked. "He's looking good, huh?" Kevin methodically ran the body brush along the roan's sides.

"Yep." Christina frowned and picked up a piece of hay to chew on. If only Jazz was showing some of that potential! Christina knew the filly was something special—she had overcome great odds and shown so much heart during her younger years

94

when her health had been so troubled. She was so beautiful now—very tall, over sixteen hands, and even the funny white splotch over her face and one ear didn't detract from her elegant lines and powerful muscle structure. But she just wasn't performing.

Ian McLean walked down the aisle. "Hi, kids," he greeted them. Walking over to True Gift, he rubbed the tall roan on his neck and forehead. "Hey, fella," he said. "How are you doing? Are you going to win the Bluegrass? You going to trample Lord Townsend in the dust?"

"It'll be a real match, all right," Kevin said with a touch of worry. "Lord's been doing real well in the prep races. But so has True."

Lord Townsend, Townsend Acres' star three-year-old, had been sired by Lord Ainsley, who years before had lost the Horse of the Year honors to Wonder's Pride. Lord Townsend's dam had been one of Wonder's foals, Townsend Princess. Now that Wonder's youngest offspring was a retired five-year-old and Wonder herself was twenty-five, Christina hardly ever went over to Townsend Acres, and the Townsends hardly ever came to Whitebrook. Which suited Christina just fine.

The only times Christina saw the Townsends now were at jumping exhibitions and three-day events—and, of course, at various racecourses when both farms had horses running. Ross still competed regularly on his new Thoroughbred,

Townsend Justice. While Christina had been desperately trying to find a decent mount for two years, Ross had his very own Thoroughbred. Over the past three years they had competed against each other many times, but Christina knew it was a matter of time before Ross and Justice blew her out of the water for good. The three times she had won against them had been sheer luck.

Now, with summer coming, the hunt clubs would all be starting their competitions. Christina and Rebecca had planned to participate in two of the smaller ones around Kentucky, but so far Christina had been unable to look ahead further than that. There was no way that she could compete at Briarsley again—not at the demanding level her age and expertise would require. She sighed.

"Have you done the algebra homework yet?" Kevin asked, putting the grooming things away. Kevin and Christina were both in eighth grade at Henry Clay Middle School and shared several classes.

"No, and I should probably get a start on our social studies project, too, since next week is going to be crazy with the race and all."

Kevin nodded. "Me too. Between working the horses in the morning, school, and my regular chores, I don't seem to have time for anything else. I'll be glad when school is out."

Christina sighed again. "You said it."

96

They sat in companionable silence on the wooden bench in front of the training barn, with Christina chewing on a piece of hay and Kevin whittling a wooden whistle for his dog, a border collie named Smoggy.

"It seems strange not to see Len sitting here," Christina said quietly, and Kevin nodded. The gentle old stable manager who had been around their whole lives had died in his sleep a year before. He hadn't been replaced. "He helped me so much with Jazz after she was born," Christina remembered. "I couldn't have done it without him."

"Yeah. He knew a lot about horses," Kevin agreed. Shading his eyes, he squinted down the long gravel driveway. "Is that Sammy's truck?"

When the truck pulled to a stop, Samantha Nelson hopped out. "Hi!" she called. Her long, wavy red hair was pulled back into a neat braid, and her green eyes were alight.

"Hey, sis," Kevin said.

Christina gave Samantha a big smile.

"How about a soda?" Samantha hinted, plopping down on the bench next to her half brother and giving him a kiss. "It's a warm day."

Christina ran to the small fridge they kept in the stable office and returned with an icy can for Samantha, one for Kevin, and one for herself. Samantha took an appreciative sip.

"Whew, it feels like summer's practically here," Samantha said, brushing some wisps of hair off her brow. "Anyway, I was going to call you this morning but got tied up. So I decided to pass by while I was out doing errands."

"Do you need some help at the stable?" Christina often lent a hand at the Nelsons' when they were running short on staff. Her work helped offset some of the expenses of her riding and dressage lessons with Tor.

Samantha shook her head. "Nope. I have something I wanted to talk to you about. One of our students is moving away and has asked us to find a home for her horse. He's a very nice Thoroughbred–Irish hunter cross, a bit over fifteen hands. His name is Jackson's Folly. Anyway, we ended up buying him, because we know we can find a good home for him. Tor thought you should come take a look at him. He's been trained in three-day eventing, and he might be better than some of the other ones you've been working with."

"Really?" Christina said excitedly.

Samantha smiled. "When you come over for your lesson tomorrow, you can try him out and see what you think. Or I can drive you over to the stable to take a look at him now."

"Are you kidding? Let's go!" Christina was already running to the large outdoor training oval where she knew her father was finishing the morning workouts. Breathlessly she told her father where she was going.

"Okay, honey. I hope this horse works out for you," her father said with a smile.

Two minutes later she was seated beside Samantha and Kevin in the pickup truck, heading to the Nelsons' stable.

"Whose horse was he?" Christina asked during the ride.

"An older girl's—Susan Bishop. You might have seen her around, though she didn't board with us."

"What's Jackson's Folly like? I can't place him."

"Folly's a nice horse," Samantha said as she drove. "I think you'll like him. He's a dapple gray, very pretty, and a good jumper. He's eight years old. Seems to have a good temperament, too."

Soon they arrived at the stable, and Christina waved to Tor, who was in the big outdoor ring conducting a class. She had a class with him tomorrow after school, in dressage. She and Kevin followed Samantha back to the stabling area. Samantha paused in front of one of the box stalls and opened the door. Christina peered in, trying to adjust to the dim light after the bright sunshine outside.

Jackson's Folly was indeed a very pretty horse, Christina saw when Samantha led him out. He looked like a small Thoroughbred, except that his neck and hindquarters were slightly heavier boned, like a hunter's. His coat was several pale shades of gray, and his mane and tail were lighter.

"Nice." Christina nodded as she studied the horse. She stepped closer to him and patted his neck. "Hey, there, fella. You're a pretty boy; yes, you are."

"Why don't you take him out and try him?" Samantha suggested. "There's no one in the back paddock right now."

"Thanks, I will."

With Kevin's help, Christina put Folly in crossties and quickly tacked him up. Then she led Folly out to the rear paddock, and Kevin opened the gate for her to go in. Samantha and Kevin watched from the fence as Christina mounted, settled in the saddle, then urged him into a walk. She put him into a trot, then a canter. He was well balanced, with a smooth gait and light, crisp movements. He responded instantly to her signals. Christina felt an instant rapport with the horse. As they rode she talked to him constantly, praising him, getting him used to the sound of her voice. When he was well warmed up, Christina took him over several low jumps, just small crossbars that were set up in the center of the paddock. Folly was eager and executed the jumps cleanly, with brisk, powerful moves.

"How'd he feel?" Samantha called as Christina rode back to the paddock gate.

"Terrific!" Christina said with a wide smile.

Samantha grinned. "Good. Maybe we've finally found you the right mount, and you two can win some show ribbons this summer."

"And beat Ross Townsend," Kevin said with a knowing look.

"Right!" Christina laughed. "Thank you so much, Sammy! I'm really excited about him—he feels great! Of course, we have a lot of work to do before we make a good team, but I think we can do it."

Samantha hugged Christina. "I'm glad, sweetie. From now on, he's your regular mount. Is your dad getting excited about the Bluegrass?"

"You know it! You'll be there, won't you?"

"Wouldn't miss it," Samantha promised.

THE BACKSIDE OF KEENELAND WAS ALIVE WITH EXCITE-ment and palpable tension the morning of the Bluegrass, one of the last big prep races before the Kentucky Derby.

"Hey, beautiful," Christina crooned, rubbing her hand gently down True Gift's nose.

"He looks good, doesn't he?" Kevin asked proudly. In Whitebrook's stabling True Gift waited quietly, and yet Christina could tell that the big, handsome colt knew today was a special day.

Early that morning Christina and Kevin had arrived at the track with Mr. Reese and the McLeans. True Gift had been brought over several days before so he could be worked on the track and get used to its feel.

This morning Christina and Kevin had groomed every shining inch of him and then stayed right outside his stall, discouraging curious onlookers from disturbing him. Now the two friends had changed into nicer clothes and were playing cards while they waited impatiently for it to be time to head to the grandstands.

Inside the stall the three-year-old roan stepped delicately back and forth, bobbing his head and stamping his powerful hindquarters. He seemed to be collecting his energy, as though he knew that this next race was his most important yet.

"Well, even if he doesn't win, he'll still go on to the Derby," Kevin said confidently. "And I'll take two cards." He put down his discards.

Christina dealt him two more cards. "Yeah," she agreed. "But it would be great if he won today too. Especially against Lord Townsend. And dealer takes one card."

Soon Mr. Reese and Kevin's father came to take True Gift to the receiving barn. A half hour later, Kevin left to meet them in the saddling ring to walk the horse until it was time for the jockey to mount. Fidel Varela, who had ridden Runaway three years before, had continued to be one of Whitebrook's regular jockeys and was riding today.

Christina made her way to Whitebrook's reserved seats in the owners' box. Although it was only mid-April, she had already attended three or four smaller races with her father. But this was the most important race by far, and she found it impossible to sit still in her seat.

Right before the race went off, Kevin joined her in the box. "There's Lord Townsend," he muttered, looking through his binoculars as the lead ponies led the racers out onto the field.

"He looks good," Christina said unenthusiastically.

"Yeah," Kevin agreed. "He's acting up a little bit, but not bad."

They both knew that frequently the excitement before a race affected the high-strung Thoroughbreds to the point that they burned out all their energy before they even got started.

"There's True," Kevin said, pointing to Fidel Varela in the blue-and-white silks of Whitebrook. Even from where they sat, the tall roan colt looked magnificent. His carriage was positively royal, Christina thought, admiring his high, dainty steps and the elegant arch of his fine neck. The sun shone on his dark red coat and glinted off Fidel's visor. A prickle of excitement skittered down Christina's spine.

Soon Christina and Kevin were joined by Samantha, Tor, Ian and Beth McLean, and Mike Reese. Everyone bustled quickly into their seats as the horses were loaded into the large starting gate.

True Gift was loaded into the number-seven position. There were twelve horses running in all, and being seventh pushed True farther over to the right than they had hoped. The buzz of excitement faded around Christina as she thought of her mother. When Ashleigh wasn't too much older than Christina was now, she'd had a horse she'd helped train, Ashleigh's Wonder, running in the Bluegrass. Wonder had won that day and then gone on to win the Kentucky Derby. Christina's face flushed with pride as she thought of it.

"And they're off!"

Christina snapped to attention as the announcer began his excited banter.

"We have some real speed horses here today, ladies and gentlemen, and they're burning up the track. Lord Townsend has taken the early lead but is fighting it out with Sweet Charity and Nybello, who are contesting the lead on the outside."

Her fists clenched at her sides, Christina watched as the horses pounded around the first turn. They had all expected Lord Townsend to be an early speed horse, so that was no surprise. True Gift had shown before that he ran off the pace until almost halfway through a race, then would pour on the speed to make a late-closing finish. Christina knew her father was confident that True would charge up toward the end to really challenge Lord Townsend, but then again, nothing was ever certain in a race.

Next to Christina her father muttered, "Get him out of there. . . ."

"And it's Lord Townsend holding on to a slim

lead over Nybello! Sweet Charity has dropped back into fourth and is losing ground. Howard's Luck is moving up into third place! True Gift is in mid-pack, still eight lengths off the pace."

Frowning, Christina kept her eyes glued to the field but reached out to take her father's hand. He squeezed it and winked at her. Now True Gift was starting to head up through the ranks, finding openings between the galloping hooves and moving into them with speed and precision. As they neared the far turn a bank of five horses momentarily blocked his way, and after a split second of hesitation Fidel Varela urged True around on the outside.

Christina heard her father grunt. "Nothing else to do," he muttered. They would have to cover more ground going around horses, but it was better than being stuck behind a solid wall and possibly not finding an opening.

A few more ground-eating strides and True Gift was clear of his competition and moving up to challenge Lord Townsend. Within seconds he was running alongside the flank of the big chestnut from Townsend Acres.

Christina jumped to her feet, yelling, "Go, True, go! Go, True, go!" On the other side of her, Kevin was screaming encouragement too.

As they watched, holding their breaths, Fidel kneaded his hands along True Gift's neck and urged him onward. But as horse and rider approached the wire it became clear that Lord Townsend was holding on and that True Gift wouldn't have quite enough ground to pass the leader. Another few yards and True would have done it, but when they swept past the finish, Lord Townsend was the winner by the barest margin.

"Lord Townsend wins by a nose!" the announcer cried. "After an impressive late run by True Gift! It's True Gift in second, and Howard's Luck in third. These horses are the ones to watch for in the Derby, ladies and gentlemen!"

Feeling deflated, Christina sank down into her seat. Kevin met her eye, and they made identical grimacing faces.

But her father and Ian McLean didn't seem too disappointed. "He made a real good showing," her dad said, patting Christina on the back. "It's a disappointment, but he still did real well, considering what he was up against. I have big hopes for the Derby."

"He put in a perfect race," Ian McLean concurred. "It was just bad luck he had to go around so many horses."

"It's a shame he didn't win," Beth McLean agreed. "But still, it was a great race." She shivered, her face glowing. "I don't think I'll ever get used to the tension, the pressure! Sometimes I can't stand it!"

Christina laughed and hugged the older woman. Beth McLean was really nice—Christina felt almost as comfortable at Kevin's house as she did at her own.

"I knew it!" Samantha crowed, also giving Beth a hug. "It's taken fifteen years, but we've finally turned you into a racing fanatic." Beth was an aerobics instructor and a physical therapist. When she had married Ian McLean and become Samantha's stepmother, she hadn't known a thing about horses.

They all laughed, then made their way down from the grandstand. Kevin rushed ahead to collect True Gift as he came off the track.

Christina headed for the backside, where she would wait while True Gift was prepared for the van to take him back home. His legs had to be rubbed down and bandaged after the race, and there were a million other details her father, Ian, and Kevin would be attending to before they headed back to Whitebrook. In the meantime she gathered up all their tack and grooming equipment and loaded their trunks.

"Christina—great race."

The friendly voice made Christina look up, and she smiled as she recognized Mandy Jarvis. Christina hadn't seen her around at the Nelsons' stable lately, but she avidly followed Mandy's career. The tall, elegant black woman had been making a name for herself, not only in America but in Europe. Christina knew Mandy intended to try out for the U.S. Olympic Equestrian Team soon.

"Thanks, Mandy. He did a great job, didn't he? And we're hoping for better in the Derby."

"I bet he'll do it for you. He looked terrific out there today."

"Thanks. Congratulations on your win last week at the Rolex Kentucky," Christina said. The Rolex was one of the most prestigious and difficult three-day events in the country. Only the very top riders could qualify, and sometimes the winners went on to join the U.S. Equestrian Team. Christina was already determined to compete in the Rolex herself, when she was old enough. *And* if she ever had the perfect mount.

"I owe it all to Bright Star," Mandy said modestly. "And of course, Samantha and Tor, for teaching me—and believing in me."

They chatted for another few moments, then a handsome young man came up and told Mandy her parents were waiting for them. Christina bid her good-bye, promising to see her the following week at the Nelsons', then turned back to her work.

"How's it feel to be second?" a taunting voice asked.

From where she crouched, loading a tack trunk, Christina narrowed her eyes. *That's all I need*, she thought sourly. *Stupid old Ross Townsend rubbing it in.*

"I guess you must be used to it, huh?" he asked.

"What do you want, Ross?" Christina asked sharply.

"Oh, nothing," he said with mock innocence. "I guess we pretty much already have everything we want. Like the better horse, for instance."

Gritting her teeth, Christina made no reply.

"So, you going to Groton?" he asked, a knowing sneer on his face. He knew she wouldn't have a mount ready for the important meet in Connecticut in June. "Justice and I are competing in intermediate sixteen-and-under. My teacher thinks we'll be pretty unbeatable."

"Goody for you," Christina said, not looking at him.

"Have you found anything to ride yet?" Ross persisted. "Why can't you just ask your dad for one of his horses, like I did with mine? I heard you have a filly out of Fleet Goddess who's a total dud on the track. Not to say she'd do any better at jumping." Ross grinned at her meanly.

Christina instinctively took a quick step closer to Ross. Without even meaning to do it, she lifted her hand to slap his cheek as hard as she could. But just at that moment, her father came around the corner of the stall.

"Chris, honey? You ready?"

Christina stopped in mid-action. After a pause she called, "Yes, Dad," not taking her eyes off Ross's horrible, good-looking face. With a final glare she stuck out her tongue at him, then turned to follow her father. She knew it was a childish

110

thing to do, but it was all she could come up with. *We're going to beat your horse next month at the Derby, Ross Townsend. Wait and see.*

During the brief ride back to Whitebrook, Christina sat silently next to her father in the cab of their pickup.

"Ross Townsend giving you a hard time?" her father finally asked, breaking the quiet.

Christina looked at him in surprise. She didn't know how much her father had overheard of her altercation with Ross.

"Oh, well . . ." she said lamely.

"I guess I hadn't really realized how much not having a decent horse has held you back all this time," he went on.

So her father *had* noticed! He had been thinking about it. "At least I have Folly now—he's doing really well."

"He's not like Justice, though." Mr. Reese looked troubled, and Christina hated to see it.

"Dad, don't worry about it. Ross doesn't get to me," she lied.

Her father shot her a smile, as though he knew it wasn't true but wasn't going to argue with her about it. It was now or never, Christina thought. This was her chance to ask her father about Jazz.

"Dad," she began hesitantly. "I've been thinking.

111

You know, I'm very serious about three-day eventing."

"I know. I've been real proud of how well you've done. Your grandma Griffen says that when your mom was your age, she was already just as determined about *racing*. You're just like her—horses are in your blood. But you've chosen a different path from hers."

Christina watched her father. Did he want her to be a jockey instead? She thought she might already be too tall.

"Yeah, I have," she agreed. "You know, Dad, Jazz Goddess isn't going to be a racer. It just doesn't look like she has it in her."

"I know. I was going to take her out of training after the Bluegrass," her father admitted. "In another year or two she'll be a nice broodmare for us."

"That's what I wanted to talk to you about," Christina said, plowing ahead. "She's not good on the flat, but she does have a big, deep chest and strong hindquarters. She's quick to learn and alert. Smart."

Her father pulled the van onto the long gravel driveway at Whitebrook, then slowed to a stop in front of the stable without saying anything. Mark Anderson, the older groom, was already there, ready to help unload True Gift. In the McLeans' cottage, Christina knew there was a post-Bluegrass party being set up.

"What I'm saying, Dad, is—I want you to let me try to train Jazz for eventing." She took a quick breath. "I mean, could I please have Jazz to train?"

Her father was still silent, looking through the truck window out into the night.

Why wasn't he saying anything? Christina wondered with dread. What was she going to do if he said no? "I've been taking care of her since she was born," Christina said desperately. "I mean, I wouldn't know until I started training her, but she has the perfect physical build to be a jumper. Haven't you noticed it? And we have such a close relationship . . . Lately I've been wishing more and more that I could retrain her—but I didn't want to ask." Her voice trailed off. Behind them, they could hear the van door being opened and the metallic thumps of True Gift's shoes walking down the ramp.

"I remember your mother telling me about how she begged for the chance to train Wonder, so many years ago," Mr. Reese said wistfully. "She had to convince Clay Townsend, her parents, everyone. And look what she did." Turning to Christina, he smiled and gently patted her hand. "She was single-minded. You remind me so much of her sometimes—the way you act, the way you look, the things that are important to you."

Without warning, tears sprang to Christina's eyes. When her father spoke so lovingly, so sadly about the mother she had never known, a pang shot

113

through Christina's heart. It was almost unbearable.

Mr. Reese straightened up and swallowed, then turned back to Christina with a wobbly grin. "Well, she had to convince all those people, but you only had to convince me. And you have."

Christina stared at him. Did he mean . . .

"She's yours, sweetie," her father said. "Here's the deal. I'll give you a year with Jazz to train her as a jumper. See if you can make something of her. But," he continued seriously, "if after a year she's still a dud for some reason, that's it. She's going into breeding. Are we clear on that?"

"Oh, yes!" Christina cried, throwing her arms around her father's neck. "Oh, Dad, thank you, thank you! I can't believe it. I know she'll do well— I know she's supposed to be a jumper. We won't let you down, I promise!"

After giving her father another tight squeeze, Christina jumped out of the truck and ran to the training barn. She let herself into Jazz's stall and hugged her horse. "Oh, Jazz, you won't believe it! It's going to be me and you from here on out! We're going to be champions, girl! I just know it!"

With an understanding whicker, Jazz gently lipped Christina's short blond hair. Sighing happily, Christina rested her head against the filly's silky black neck. "This is the beginning, Jazz," she whispered. "This is the beginning of everything."

8

FOR THE NEXT THREE WEEKS, EVERY MOMENT THAT Christina wasn't at school, sleeping, or training with Jackson's Folly, she was with Jazz. She bounced out of bed at four thirty every morning and raced through her regular chores, mucking out stalls, grooming horses, and taking care of her share of the housework as well. Then she would work Jazz for almost an hour before school.

After much advice and heartfelt discussion between her, Samantha, and Tor, Christina had settled into a routine. Because Jazz was used to running only counterclockwise around a track, Christina needed to increase her suppleness and balance. To do this she worked the filly on a longe line, circling her clockwise, strengthening her muscles and improving the fluidness of her gait on the right lead. On the track, Jazz had run primarily on her left lead.

115

By the end of the first week in May, she was riding Jazz over cavalletti placed low on the ground.

"She's working really great," Christina said enthusiastically as she and Rebecca waited for the school bus one day after school. "She's just so smart, so quick to catch on. And I don't know—maybe I'm just kidding myself, but she seems eager and interested. More than she ever was when she was in training to flat race."

"Maybe it's because she's working only with you," Rebecca pointed out reasonably. "You two have been practically joined at the nose since she was born. It only makes sense that she would put out her best effort for you."

Beaming, Christina said, "It's so exciting. I think by next summer we'll be ready to compete. This winter I'll do a lot of dressage with her, and we can take her out on the cross-country trails, too."

Kevin came up then, swinging his backpack by one strap. The yellow school bus wasn't far behind, and the three of them managed to find seats together in the back.

"Have you registered for the Blucher Farms meet?" Kevin asked them when they were seated and the bus had taken off. He sat back and brushed his dark red hair off his face.

Both girls nodded. "It isn't till the end of the month," Christina said. "I feel like I'm pretty ready with Folly."

"I hope I do as well on Marbella. Tor seems to think we're ready," Rebecca said. "But I'm getting a little more worried about my school grades now. Finals are only three weeks away."

"You'll do fine," Christina reassured her. "I'm going to start cramming two weeks before, but it's going to be hard since Blucher Farms is right in the middle of it. Can you guys believe that we're going to be in high school next year?"

Rebecca grinned. "I'm glad we'll all be going to Henry Clay. Guess who else is going? Kyle Parrish. He is *so* cute."

Christina and Kevin exchanged a grin.

"Oh, thank heavens," Kevin said teasingly. "We can all relax now that Kyle's going."

Rebecca swatted him playfully.

"You guys must be excited about the Derby this weekend," she said, obviously trying to change the subject. "How's True Gift?"

"He's never been better," Kevin said. "He's going to beat Lord Townsend this time, I know it."

"Oh, that reminds me," Christina said to Rebecca, standing up to get off at her stop. "Dad says there's a Derby ticket with your name on it. Want to go?"

Rebecca almost fell out of her seat. "Watch the Kentucky Derby from the owners' box?" she shrieked. "Are you kidding? Try to stop me!"

Laughing, Christina followed Kevin down the

bus aisle. "Good. We'll pick you up on Friday afternoon after school. Dad will already be in Louisville with True, to get him settled."

"Fantastic!" Rebecca yelled out of her bus window, waving happily at them.

Two days before the Derby, huge torrents of rain soaked the green Kentucky fields. It had been an unusually dry spring so far, and in some ways the rain was welcome, because the clover-covered paddocks would be refreshed and covered anew with sweet, crunchy grass. And the rain washed off all the dry, red-brown dust that had been covering buildings, cars, and horses for the last month.

"But for it to rain now!" Christina agonized, gazing out the training stable door to watch the sheets of water come pouring out of the sky.

"It's supposed to be dry tomorrow," Kevin said, trying to sound optimistic.

"Yeah, but even if it's dry tomorrow and the next day, how much can the track at Louisville recover before the race?" Christina asked gloomily. "True Gift hates running on a muddy track. I wonder if Lord Townsend does too."

Kevin shook his head and shrugged. "You know True will do his best. Don't worry about it. Why don't you come over tonight and help me study for Mrs. Spinner's history test tomorrow?"

"I don't know if I'll be any help," Christina said

gloomily. "Between working with both Jazz and Jackson's Folly, and worrying about True Gift and Lord Townsend and stupid Ross Townsend, I feel like I'm losing my mind."

Kevin laughed and threw a handful of clean straw at her. "You have to lighten up. You know what they say: it's only a race."

"Oh, right," Christina said sarcastically. "I'm sure you really believe that. 'It's only a race,'" she mimicked. "It's the Kentucky Derby, you idiot!"

Kevin laughed again.

On Friday afternoon after school Samantha drove Christina, Rebecca, and Kevin over to Louisville, about an hour and a half away. While it had been cloudy all day, it hadn't actually rained any more. On the other hand, there hadn't been any bright sunshine to dry out the track, either.

That night Christina, Rebecca, and Samantha shared a motel room not too far from the track. The entire place was devoted to horse-racing people, quite a few of whom Christina recognized. Resisting the urge to stay up late talking, they all turned in. Right before Christina was about to fall asleep, she thought of her mother. What had her mother thought about the night before Wonder was going to run in the Kentucky Derby? She must have been so excited, and scared—and yet confident. In the darkness of the motel room, Christina smiled. She thought she understood what her mother had felt, and it made her feel very close to her right now.

The next morning they were up at five to get to the backside in plenty of time for all the action. By the time they were settled outside True Gift's stall, drinking juice out of paper cups and sharing a bag of doughnuts with Kevin and Mark Anderson, the sun was rising on a clear, brilliantly sunny day.

"True's been training really well since the Bluegrass," Christina told Rebecca as they finally followed Samantha to their reserved seats for the Derby. The day had flown by, and the Derby was set to go off in just ten minutes. At the owners' box, Christina introduced Rebecca to her grandparents, Derek and Elaine Griffen. Tor had driven up that morning, and he greeted them cheerfully. Beth McLean settled next to him on the other side, anxiously adjusting her wide-brimmed, flower-covered hat.

"I got it special, just for today," she confessed, pinning it firmly to her short blond hair. Christina smiled at her.

"I guess True wasn't able to train too well on the track this week, huh?" Rebecca murmured after they had settled into their seats.

Christina shook her head. "Not with all that rain."

The two girls examined their programs. It was a huge field of fourteen horses, made up of all the best three-year-olds in the country. After the Bluegrass, Lord Townsend was the odds-on favorite. Christina only hoped True Gift wouldn't get stuck behind a wall of horses again and that the sloppy track wouldn't bother him too much, but anything could happen. A lot would depend on how he broke from the number-five position he'd drawn and what kind of traffic he encountered on the field.

Minutes before the race, the crowd's enthusiasm was explosive. Christina was afraid the cheering clamor would upset the horses. She was already on the edge of her seat but was trying to distract herself by gossiping with Rebecca about all the racing people she could see in the stands. Soon they were joined by Christina's father and Ian McLean, who had been with the colt until the last minute, as usual.

With her binoculars, Christina could see Ross Townsend in the Townsend Acres seating with his parents and his grandfather. They all looked pretty smug. With a sick feeling in her stomach, Christina turned her attention to the field.

The escort ponies led the horses out onto the track for the post parade and their warm-up jog around the track to the starting gate. Christina's stomach tightened. Then the horses were loaded. One horse, a French colt, was bucking and acting up. Gate attendants were trying to grab his bridle.

Christina saw True Gift being loaded into the number-five position. She looked up at her father, and he smiled down at her, though there were tense lines around his mouth.

One after another the horses were put into the starting gate. Lord Townsend had already loaded into the three spot, which was good for him, since he would just immediately leap out to the front anyway.

Then came the big moment. The gates broke and fourteen sleek, powerful Thoroughbreds leaped out onto the track, their jockeys hunched low over their withers. The track was still damp, as Christina had feared, but it didn't seem to be thick mud soup.

As expected, Lord Townsend bolted to the front, but two other horses were right by his side, challenging him for an early lead. Fighting to stay in front, the colt shot into a higher gear, setting faster fractions than normal. Christina knew that it could mean the big chestnut would run out of steam before the end of the race. But it was good news for True Gift—the faster the early fractions, the easier it would be for him to come up from behind and make his fast closing finish.

Within thirty seconds all the horses except the ones in the lead were covered with a fine coating of red dirt, kicked up by hooves churning down the loose track. True Gift was running easily and smoothly about ten lengths behind the leaders. The announcer kept up his fast-talking commentary, but Christina couldn't pay attention. Every bit of her was focused on the field of horses, galloping around the first turn as though in silent slow motion.

Lord Townsend was by now locked into a speed duel in earnest, and already Christina could tell the pace was showing on him. His neck was dark and lathered with sweat, but his powerful legs churned on. The field roared down the backstretch, nearing the far turn, and the jockey in the green-and-gold Townsend Acres silks asked Lord Townsend for more speed. The horse turned up a notch and began to pull away from his competition.

Christina was chewing her lip by now. This was the moment when True Gift would either start to accelerate and catch up or lag behind and finish among the last. That was the trouble with a late closer—some days they simply didn't click in. Christina prayed this wouldn't be one of those days.

Moments later she let out a shout as True Gift picked up his pace and began to move forward like a freight train, passing horses right and left. Though there were fourteen horses in the field, they were spread out along the track, leaving openings for True Gift. With rising excitement Christina thought that he made the other horses look as though they were standing still as he roared by them.

"Come on, True! Go, boy, go!" Christina and Rebecca screamed. They were on their feet, jumping up and down and waving their arms. The crowd around them was roaring, and the announcer could barely be heard.

By the time the lead horses swept past the

sixteenth pole, True Gift was rushing up to challenge Lord Townsend, who was visibly tiring. Looking back under his arm, the Townsend jockey saw True Gift and went for his whip, but it was too late! True Gift flashed by Lord Townsend at the last second and powered under the wire a length in the lead!

Then the crowd was on its feet, screaming and jumping up and down. Christina hugged Rebecca, then her father, then Kevin, then everyone else within reach.

"We did it!" her father was yelling. "True Gift did it! What a horse! What a race!" The whole Whitebrook contingent were dancing with joy, and happy tears were running down Samantha's face. It was the first Derby winner for Whitebrook, and by a colt who had been born and bred on the farm. This would mean higher stud fees, better breeding horses, more recognition . . . It was a much-needed shot in the arm for the small training stable.

Breathlessly Christina followed her father down to the winner's circle, where True Gift was waiting, already draped with his blanket of roses. Although his coat was wet with sweat and he whoofed a bit tiredly, he still tossed his elegant head proudly, as though to say, "I told you I could do it." Laughing, Christina threw her arms around the big colt and hugged him, then congratulated Fidel Varela, who looked dazed and happy. Mr. McLean and Mike Reese posed for the cameras and began to answer hastily shouted questions from reporters and the television anchor.

Christina beamed until her face felt sore. She suddenly had a real understanding of everything her mother had worked so hard for during her short life. Being a champion, helping a horse perform its best, standing here in the winner's circle—it was worth everything they had to go through to get there. *I understand now, Mom,* Christina thought, bemusedly gazing at all the snapping flashbulbs. *It's the most wonderful feeling in the world. No wonder you never stopped winning.*

That night there was a big postrace party at a fancy hotel in Louisville. There was a huge buffet of food, and a band, and more reporters. That afternoon Christina and Rebecca had helped settle True Gift in his stall, waiting while Christina's father and Ian McLean examined him thoroughly for lameness or soreness. But he seemed to have come out of the race okay.

To Christina's delight, they had run into Ross Townsend along the backside. As they walked past to get to the Whitebrook stabling, they had seen him leaning against Lord Townsend's stall. He had looked angry and depressed. Christina was about to make a snide comment to get him back for all his earlier nastiness when she noticed that Ross's parents, Brad and Lavinia Townsend, were apparently having an argument nearby. Their voices were raised, and Lavinia was waving her arms in the air. Six-year-old Laura was clinging to her mother's skirt and crying. Although Christina had been about to rub in the Whitebrook victory, when she saw the unhappy family scene, she bit back her words. Ross seemed embarrassed, and for a split second, Christina actually felt a little sorry for him. She and Rebecca hurried by.

Now the two girls were sitting at their own table with Kevin, who was on his third plate from the buffet.

"These little roast beef sandwiches are great!" he said enthusiastically, holding one up in demonstration. At thirteen, Kevin had just started to catch up to Christina in the height department, and it left him with a constantly ravenous appetite.

"I'm going back for more dessert," Rebecca said, pushing back her chair. "Anyone want anything?"

"Not me," Christina said. Across the room, her father was toasting Ian McLean with a glass of champagne. Christina knew that soon the two men would head back to the stabling area at Churchill Downs to check on True Gift one last time. And tomorrow they would all drive back to Lexington.

Suddenly the excitement of the day caught up with her, and Christina felt very tired. As soon as she got home tomorrow, she decided, she would take Jazz Goddess out for a long jog over the cross-country trails. In just a few weeks school would be over, and then Christina could devote her time to training with her two horses: Jazz Goddess and Jackson's Folly. But right now, she had to help her dad celebrate Whitebrook's biggest win.

Smiling, Christina caught her father's eye across the room and raised her glass of punch to him. It was going to be a great summer, and she could hardly wait.

9

OKAY, FOLLY, HERE'S A WATER JUMP—YOU LIKE THESE . . . one, two, three . . . GO! Christina squeezed with her legs, and Folly bounded over the fence and water jump easily, then headed down the winding cross-country trail through the woods. During this second event at the Blucher Farms meet, they would have to jump seven different obstacles. Christina knew that a judge waited by each jump, and points would be deducted if Folly balked or refused a jump, ticked it, or knocked it down. The obstacles they were jumping now were more rustic than the show-jumps: some of them were made out of logs with the bark still on, or were painted to look like stone walls or a pile of branches.

Folly took the jumps easily and stayed focused and collected during the ride. By the time they rode out of the woods and up to the final judges' panel, Christina knew they had done their best.

The Blucher Farms meet, which took place during the last weekend of May, was one of Christina's favorite competitions. Yesterday she and Rebecca had competed in dressage; today was cross-country in the morning, followed this afternoon by show-jumping. Three-day events, even when they were scheduled over just two days, always followed this pattern: dressage, to make sure both horse and rider had been well schooled in the fundamentals; cross-country, to demonstrate speed, endurance, and jumping ability; and then show-jumping. show-jumping always came after cross-country so that the judges could see if the horse still had something left after the very demanding cross-country. If a horse could still execute difficult jumps in the ring after putting out its full effort on cross-country, then it was a special horse indeed. And the precision and obedience it demonstrated in the show ring would speak volumes about its training.

Both Christina and Folly and Rebecca and Marbella had done very well so far—if they rode clean during show-jumping, they each had a chance to win a ribbon.

For show-jumping Christina changed back into a regular riding habit. When it was her turn, she rode into the ring, saluted the judges, then heeled Folly into a collected canter toward the first jump, a single fence.

Okay, Folly, keep it tight, look ahead, and it's a double gate . . . three, two, one, squeeze. And they were up and over. Immediately Christina looked ahead to the next jump, which she knew would be an oxer. She counted strides mentally, reviewing the pattern of the course in her mind. Keeping Folly collected in an even-paced, steady canter, she turned him and headed for the oxer. As usual, the horse responded nimbly and alertly, and then with a squeeze of her legs Christina gave him the signal. He bounded over cleanly and landed with a light thud on the trimmed lawn on the other side.

Last one, boy. We can do it. It's a parallel combination. Just go UP . . . Instinctively Christina squeezed at exactly the right moment, and the dappled gray stretched his forelegs out to sail easily over the wide jump. Then his hindquarters thundered down and they were done.

Christina had gone clean! She circled Folly and rode him over to where Tor was waiting.

"Terrific, Chris!" he congratulated her, then held Folly's bridle so she could dismount. "I would have maybe let him out a tiny bit before the oxer, but anyway, you did a great job."

Christina couldn't help laughing. Tor always had a word of advice or some small correction to offer, no matter how well she had done. The times he had beamed and said, "Perfect!" she could count on one hand. But she was glad he paid so much attention to every nuance of her performance. It was the only way she'd get better.

Rebecca ran over and gave her a hug. "Good ride, Chris! You two looked fabulous out there." Rebecca and Marbella had already gone and had jumped clean.

Christina smiled at her friend, then took off her hard hat, which was hot under the late-spring sun. "Thanks. Folly's been working really well. It's a relief to be finished."

Nodding, Rebecca said, "Yeah. Now we don't have to worry about competing again until Kentucky Riders at the end of August."

"Uh-huh. We just have to worry about getting through school finals, and then graduation. That's all," Christina said teasingly.

It was the first semi-big show she had competed in with Folly, and he was proving to be a terrific mount. More than ever Christina wished she'd had enough time to train with him, enter more shows, and get enough points awarded to qualify for Groton in late June, or Briarsley. But still, it was a nice start today, with Blucher Farms. Kentucky Riders would be a pretty important show, and she had decided that if she and Folly did well there, she would go ahead and enter the Newgate meet, at Huntington, West Virginia. It was bigger than Kentucky Riders or Blucher Farms, and it had a good reputation. If she did well there, she would be in a decent position to start the following spring meets. Newgate took place the second weekend in October.

After the show-jumping competition had been judged, all the scores were added up: dressage, cross-country, and show-jumping. Eagerly Christina waited with other riders in the advanced thirteen-and-under group, hoping and praying that perhaps she had won a ribbon. Slowly the judge went through the list, awarding fourth place, then third. When they announced "Christina Reese" in second place and came over to pin a red ribbon on Folly's bridle, Christina smiled happily.

"Thank you," she said, shaking the head judge's hand. "Thank you very much." Gazing through the crowd, she caught her dad's eye where he waited behind the fence rails with the rest of the crowd. She pointed to her red ribbon, and he beamed and gave her a thumbs-up. Then she turned to Folly and kissed his soft gray nose. "Thank you, boy," she whispered. "You really put your heart into it today—you're a great partner. And next time I bet we'll do even better. Thanks." Folly whoofed gently and stamped his leg. Then a photographer came up to take her picture with Folly, and Christina smiled.

A week later Christina and her friends gradu-ated from eighth grade. By cramming frantically both the week before and the week after the

Blucher Farms meet, Christina had managed to do well in her classes—only one *C* and mostly *B*'s, with an *A* in English. In the white dress that Samantha had helped her find, Christina followed her classmates down the aisles of the middle school auditorium and up onto the stage. She could barely pick out her father and her grandparents in the audience. A feeling of déjà vu came over her as her name was called and she rose to take her diploma. *It's almost like winning a ribbon*, she thought giddily. Then she was shaking the principal's hand and murmuring "Thank you" as flashbulbs popped in the audience. It was hard to believe that next fall she would be a high school student.

Afterward she, her dad, and Grandma and Grandpa Griffen went out for dinner at one of Lexington's fanciest restaurants. They were going to meet the McLeans and Samantha and Tor back at the farmhouse for dessert, since Kevin had just graduated too. But now it was just the four of them.

"I was so proud of you, sweetheart," Grandma Griffen said. "You looked so beautiful in your dress. I hope we took enough pictures."

Christina grinned. "It sure *felt* like you took enough."

"And she made pretty good grades, too," her father said proudly. "She was twelfth in her class."

"Well, now you can relax a little, after all your hard work," her grandfather added. "What are

133

your plans for the summer? Are you in a lot of competitions?"

Christina shook her head. "No. I won't even come close to qualifying for a lot of the big ones. The only other one I'm really planning on is Kentucky Riders at the end of August. If I do well there, I'll try for Newgate in October. In the meantime, I'm just going to be training Jazz and working on my equitation with Folly."

"I hope you'll have some time to help me out a little," her father put in. "I need you to ride some horses in their morning workouts."

"Sure, Dad," Christina said eagerly. "I'd love it. Now that I'm not in school and don't have to worry about flunking all my classes, it feels like I'll finally have time for everything!"

Her father and grandparents laughed at her optimism.

"It was a shame about True Gift and the Preakness," Derek Griffen told Christina's father, changing the subject. The colt had bruised his hoof a few days before the second race in the Triple Crown, and so they had been forced to scratch him.

"Yeah," Mr. Reese agreed. "But we're still aiming him at the Belmont in New York next week. He's been training so well that I still have my hopes up for two jewels of the Triple Crown."

"We'll be pulling for you," Elaine Griffen promised. "Now, I want to talk about taking Christina to

Maine later this summer. Grandpa and I have rented a cottage for two weeks, and we'd love to have you join us for a few days—when you're not too busy."

"Oh, Grandma, I'd love to!" Christina exclaimed. "Just tell me when."

Christina was up very early the next day, her first official day of summer vacation. She loved waking up so early, before it was even light out. As she dressed hurriedly in breeches and a T-shirt, she felt a wave of peacefulness come over her. The world was still asleep: birds were quiet in their nests, crickets were buried in the ground, even the trees seem to rustle more quietly. As she crept downstairs, she wondered if her mother had shared the same feelings.

In the kitchen, Christina grabbed an apple and a glass of juice. She heard her father's alarm clock go off above her, then it was silenced. Christina grinned. Her dad would be out in the barns in a few minutes. She let herself out the back door and crossed the quiet, tidy stable yard to the training barn.

The very first hour of the morning was always Christina's favorite time to be in the barn. The horses were just waking up, and the barn echoed with contented whoofs and sighs and slight stamps of hooves. The barn cats, a large black-and-white female named Delaney and an even larger marmalade tom named Muffin, came scampering down the middle aisle in the hopes of having some milk from the office fridge.

Chuckling, Christina poured them a saucer, then headed back to check on Jazz. As usual, Jazz had heard and identified Christina's footsteps and was already looking over the top of her stall door.

"Good morning, girl," Christina said, rubbing the filly's nose and dropping a kiss on the softest part. Quickly she mucked out Jazz's stall, removing all the soiled bedding and replacing it with clean, sweet-smelling straw. Then she groomed Jazz thoroughly until she gleamed, and finally Christina gave Jazz her morning hay.

While Jazz ate, Christina mucked out her share of the other stalls. She was soon joined by Kevin and Mark Anderson and Eddie Wilcox, the two grooms. They worked with easy familiarity, calling hello to Mike Reese and Ian McLean as the two older men began making their rounds.

If only I never had to go to school again, Christina thought, wheeling a barrow full of dirty straw to the compost heap out back. *I can't wait until I'm out of college and can just do this full time.* Although she wasn't even in high school yet, Christina already harbored secret longings of skipping college and going right into the horse-world life. But she knew her father would never agree in a million years. Both her parents had gone to college, and Christina knew she would have to also. It was going to be frustrating to have one more thing come between her and her horses.

By now the sun was up, and it was a breezy, sunny, almost-summer day. In these first days of June, the temperature rarely got above eighty-five, and it usually was clear, with little humidity to make everyone irritable and sticky. *In short, a perfect day to work my favorite horse,* Christina thought.

"Okay, girl," she said to Jazz, putting the filly in crossties so she could be tacked up. "Are you ready for a great work today?"

The filly whickered and delicately stepped her hindquarters around, as though to show her enthusiasm. Christina laughed, and ten minutes later they were trotting in figure eights around the training paddock.

That day began a summertime pattern for Christina and Jazz. Each day Christina worked the filly twice—once in the morning, to develop her suppleness and balance and to practice dressage, and once in the afternoon, where they built up stamina on the long, winding cross-country trails in the woods in back of Whitebrook.

In the morning, in addition to riding Jazz in figure eights and serpentines, she worked the filly on the longe line. Until now, most of Jazz's training had been geared toward simply running as fast as possible. Now Christina had to work on sharpening

Jazz's reactions, tightening her turning abilities, and getting her used to the quick changes of pace that show-jumping would require.

Christina was careful to end every lesson on a good note so that Jazz would continue to feel enthusiastic about her training program.

In between these morning and afternoon workouts, Christina took classes at the Nelsons' stable on Folly, working on increasingly difficult jump courses and more sophisticated dressage.

From four thirty in the morning to seven o'clock at night, Christina ate, worked, and breathed horses. It was heaven on earth.

At the end of the first week of June, Christina, Rebecca, Kevin, Beth McLean, Samantha, and Tor all gathered around the large TV set in the McLeans' farmhouse. It was the day of the Belmont, and True Gift had been vanned up five days before. While her father and Ian McLean were gone, Christina had been staying with Beth and Kevin.

"Pass the popcorn, please," Christina said, plopping in front of the TV. Eagerly they watched all the prerace hoopla, and then everyone groaned as if on cue when Brad Townsend was interviewed.

Then it was race time. Christina's eyes were glued to the screen as the starting gates broke and twelve Thoroughbreds bolted onto the track. Hundreds of years of breeding had gone into the sleek animals powering down the field, and it showed in every finely carved inch of them, Christina thought with excitement. Though of course she was pulling for True Gift one hundred percent, Christina couldn't help being impressed by a brave little filly called Darby's Baby. It was clear she was putting everything she had into the race.

Next to Christina on the floor, Kevin surged forward as True Gift began to make his usual late closing run toward the finish. Just as he had at the Kentucky Derby, True Gift seemed unstoppable as he roared up the backstretch, passing horses right and left. They cheered as he swept by Lord Townsend, who was pulled up moments later by his jockey. Then Christina held her breath as True Gift thundered under the wire—an easy winner by three lengths!

"He won it!" Christina yelled, bouncing up and down on the floor where she sat. "True Gift won the Belmont! Two races of the Triple Crown!" Everyone was clapping and whistling and slapping high fives. She knew her father would be walking on air—this was really fantastic news for the farm.

"But what's wrong with Lord Townsend?" Rebecca asked, pointing at the TV. It was clear that the horse was favoring his right front leg.

"It doesn't look good," Kevin said. "I sure hope he hasn't fractured a bone."

"That would be awful," Christina said somberly. "His jockey's dismounting." But the camera moved away from the scene of the injured horse and focused on the winner's circle.

"Oh, look, they're interviewing your dad," Beth said, turning up the sound. Mike Reese stood in the winner's circle with Ian McLean at his side. True Gift was proudly wearing his blanket of flowers and was tossing his head temperamentally.

"The colt put in a great race," Christina's father was saying. "We're really thrilled with his win. It's a shame he didn't have a chance to show his stuff in the Preakness."

"Do you think you would have won if Lord Townsend hadn't come up lame?" one reporter asked.

"Yes, I do," Mr. Reese said firmly. "It's a shame about Lord Townsend—we'll all be hoping for the best for him. He put in a great race. But even so, I think our colt is the better horse."

With that the reporter wrapped up his closing comments.

Christina turned the volume back down with a worried look. "I hope Lord's injury isn't serious," she said. "But I'm really glad we won."

Her father called that night, and after Christina had excitedly congratulated her father, she asked about Lord Townsend.

"He fractured a bone in his ankle," her father said. "It's not life threatening, but he'll be sidelined for some time, and there's a possibility he won't race again."

"That's really too bad," Christina said. For an instant she felt a twinge of sympathy for Ross and his family. She knew how she'd feel if one of her father's horses were injured.

Mike Reese, Ian McLean, and True Gift came back two days later to much fanfare, and then life settled down again for the moment. Christina worked with Jazz as usual. Things with the filly didn't always go perfectly, however. While Jazz was bright and eager to learn, it took time to undo the rhythm of training for flat racing and get her used to a whole new form of moving and working. At times Jazz was confused about what was expected of her. But at three years old she was considerably younger than three-day-event horses usually were, and Christina would have plenty of time to work with her.

Sometimes Tor or Samantha came to Whitebrook to help Christina school Jazz. With Tor's help, Christina soon had Jazz trotting over very low crossbars, and then some low rails. All horses had a natural ability to jump, Christina knew, but it was important to train them to jump properly to avoid risk of injury to themselves or their rider. And of course the real test would be to see if Jazz actually enjoyed jumping and would head out to a course with interest and eagerness.

"She's looking good," Tor called one day in the

beginning of July. "You've done a good job with getting her evened out. Her gaits look nicer no matter what direction she turns."

Christina beamed with pride. "Thanks. It's all those figure eights and serpentines. I've been amazed at how quickly she picks things up. She's great on cross-country, too. Like she was made for it."

While Tor watched, Christina put the filly through her paces, riding her around the small, simple jump course she had set up in the mid-size ring. There were only four jumps, and they were all pretty low—not over two feet high.

Jazz cantered smoothly around the ring, then Christina aimed her for a single horizontal pole. They flew over it. Then there was a wide turn to the left, followed by a crossbar. No problem there. Christina was counting strides and gave the filly a squeeze when it was time to jump. The wind felt warm against Christina's face, and she could feel a trickle of sweat run down her back from the hot sun.

The third jump was another crossbar, and they cleared it with at least six inches to spare. Christina was thrilled to be doing so well with Samantha and Tor watching. Mentally she made a note to go around and raise all the jumps. At this rate, Jazz would be jumping a regulation course in no time!

Keeping her eyes focused between the filly's ears, one black, one white, Christina aimed Jazz toward the last jump, which was a small, white-painted vertical. They had jumped it every day for the past week.

As they approached the jump, there was a sudden crashing sound to their left, as if a pile of metal feed pails had tumbled to the ground. The noise was enough to startle Jazz, and she suddenly stopped dead in confusion and fear.

Caught unawares, Christina went sailing over Jazz's head, to land in an embarrassed heap on the other side of the jump. Right away Christina knew that she was okay except for her wounded pride, but Jazz had reared up on her hind legs. Her front hooves landed heavily and she took off around the ring, thoroughly spooked.

Christina was on her hands and knees, trying to get her breath back, but Tor and Samantha had already hopped the fence and were chasing Jazz down. In another moment they had caught her, and Tor began to soothe her while Samantha ran to Christina.

"I'm okay," Christina gasped, trying to suck in a dry breath. "What was that noise?"

"I don't know, but it scared the daylights out of Jazz. Are you sure you're all right?" Samantha asked worriedly.

"I'm fine." Christina scrambled up and anxiously ran to where Tor was holding Jazz. "Hey, girl—easy now, easy," she said soothingly.

Fortunately the filly hadn't hurt herself during her mad little gallop.

"It's okay," Christina said, stroking Jazz's neck. "I know you're frightened, but I'm here. Everything's going to be okay now." Christina smoothed the shining black hair with her fingers. "It wasn't your fault, girl. I don't blame you one bit. What do you say we give it another try?"

Christina knew it was important not to end the lesson on a bad note, so once Jazz was fully settled down again, she remounted and schooled the filly for another half hour until all memory of Jazz's scare had disappeared. That night she soaked in a hot tub, grimacing at the bruises she knew would be much worse the next day. But it was all part of the game.

10

THE HOT AUGUST SUN BEAT DOWN ON CHRISTINA AS SHE
sat tall in the saddle, looking straight ahead between Jazz's alert ears. Mentally she pictured a single string running from her head through her
shoulders, to her hip and down through her heel.
The string had to be perfectly in line. In Jazz's
mouth, the bit was in the correct place, and the
reins led back in a smooth arc to meet with
Christina's hands as if they were one.

Silently Christina pressed one knee against
Jazz's side, trying to keep the motion small and
precise yet not obvious to Samantha, who was
watching from the top of the fence rail. Obediently Jazz stepped away from the pressure with a
small sideways motion. Then, with the slightest
touch of her hand against the filly's neck,
Christina gave the signal to walk forward and

145

turn to the right. Jazz stepped smoothly forward.

"Bravo," Samantha cried, clapping. "This is unbelievable. I can't believe how much progress you've made with the filly in just four months!"

In another week and a half the summer would be over, and school would begin. Christina would be joining Rebecca and Kevin in ninth grade at Henry Clay High. Just a few weeks before, Christina had spent a long weekend in Maine with Grandma and Grandpa Griffen. It had been great to go swimming and sailing and fishing with them. The change of scenery had been a real treat. But even while she was having fun, Christina had been wondering what Jazz was doing and thinking about the lessons she would continue with the filly when she returned home.

"She's a quick study," Christina said with a smile. "And working her every day has helped. I also think she's just about the smartest horse I've ever known. Aren't you, girl?" As Christina patted her neck, Jazz Goddess raised her head and whickered.

Samantha laughed. "She knows it, too." She hopped off the fence and opened the gate for Christina to walk Jazz through on their way to the barn. "Tor says that you and Folly are ready for Kentucky Riders this weekend."

Nodding, Christina said, "I'm looking forward to it. He's a terrific little horse. I've been glad to have him all summer."

"Are you in advanced thirteen-and-under or intermediate sixteen-and-under?" Samantha asked, naming the two levels Christina was eligible for.

They entered the barn, and Christina began to rub Jazz down with towels to prevent her from catching a chill. "Well, after a lot of thought, I decided to go with the advanced thirteen-and-under," she told Samantha. "This is the last summer I'll be eligible for it—I'll turn fourteen this December. And since I wasn't able to compete very much this year, I decided to go out with a bang instead of a whimper."

"Good for you," Samantha said, plopping down on a hay bale. Absently she scratched behind Delaney's ears. The barn cat had come sauntering up when she heard their voices. "If you'd like, I'll take a couple days off and go with you, okay?"

Christina looked up with shining eyes. "Oh, Sammy, I would love it. Thanks so much! Kevin is going as my groom, but I need all the help I can get. Dad and I will pick you up when we come to get Jackson's Folly, early Saturday morning."

"It's a date," Samantha promised.

Two months later, the early-October wind whipped against Christina's cheeks as she and Jazz thundered down a winding path through the woods in back of Whitebrook. The sun was just starting to go down, but Christina thought she had time for one more jump before the dim light would make the ride too dangerous.

"Come on, Jazz, girl!" she cried as the big Thoroughbred pounded up a small hill. Christina's father had set up a large post-and-rail fence at the top, and Christina prepared herself for Jazz's flying leap. At the right moment Christina squeezed with her legs, and Jazz sprang up and over to land gracefully on the other side.

"Yes!" Christina cried, a feeling of supreme happiness washing over her. "Jazz, you're the best! I love you!"

These long cross-country practices were all Christina could fit in afternoons, now that school had begun and the sun was setting earlier. She still worked Jazz every morning before school, but she missed summer, when she could take more time with the filly. She looked forward to the weekends when she schooled Jazz in the important, detailed work of dressage.

Keeping Jazz in an easy canter, Christina turned the tall filly and headed back down the hill. At the base of the hill, circling her mount at a smooth trot, was Rebecca. She had borrowed one of Mr. Reese's pleasure horses for this after-school ride with Christina.

"You two are amazing!" Rebecca said excitedly when Christina was in hearing distance. She turned her gelding, and the four of them slowed to a walk and headed back down the trail toward

Whitebrook. "I swear, Chris, Jazz looks better every time I see her. She just seems . . . unstoppable."

Christina laughed. "She feels that way to me, too. It's hard to believe she was such a dud when Dad was training her on the flat. But her dressage is terrific, her show-jumping is great, and her cross-country can't be beat! I bet next year during the summer meets, Ross won't know what hit him."

"That would sure be a nice change," Rebecca said dryly, "after Kentucky Riders, back in August." Christina had come in second at that regional show. Ross had come in first and had lorded it over Christina revoltingly. Rebecca had been in sixth place.

"Don't remind me." Christina groaned. "I'm still burned up about it." Second place had been pretty disappointing. It had been a long time since she'd won a blue ribbon, and she was starting to feel as if she might be second best forever. She would never make it to the Olympics at this rate! She couldn't wait until Jazz was ready to compete.

Rebecca shrugged. "You'll do better at Newgate. How are you feeling about it?"

"I can't wait," Christina said, smiling. She turned Jazz and headed her between the white-painted fences of the back paddocks of Whitebrook. "I'm glad we have one more meet before winter. What about you?"

"Wouldn't miss it. Oh, how'd you do on that English test Tuesday?"

"An eighty-eight. English has always been my best subject. I like Ms. Hawkins, too. The stuff we're studying in ninth grade seems a lot more interesting than what we did in eighth grade, don't you think?"

Rebecca nodded. "Except civics, of course."

"Yeah. Civics is totally lame."

Christina's father was heading out of the barn when the girls walked up with their mounts. "Have a nice ride?"

"Sure did. Jazz took that jump on top of the hill like it was nothing," Christina boasted. "She's incredible."

Mr. Reese smiled and patted Jazz's flank. "I'll be the first to admit that she's made remarkable strides in her training," he said. "You've done a great job with her. She really looks like an eventer."

"Thanks, Dad," Christina said, her cheeks flushing with pride. She respected her father's opinion immensely, and it warmed her all over to know that he approved of how she had trained Jazz.

The following weekend, Christina's alarm went off at four in the morning. Huntington was two hours away, so they had to leave in plenty of time to get there and get Folly warmed up before Christina's dressage program began. Hurriedly she threw on a pair of jeans and a sweatshirt, then raced downstairs.

Half an hour later, the McLeans' family-size

minivan pulled up at the Nelsons' stable. Christina's father had borrowed the McLeans' car because the Whitebrook pickup couldn't hold himself, Christina, Rebecca, Kevin, and Samantha. The minivan easily pulled Whitebrook's two-horse trailer.

Samantha was waiting for them outside. Rebecca and Christina ran to the barn to collect their mounts. In no time Rebecca was leading Marbella, and Christina had Folly, and they were heading out to the trailer. As they walked in the dim stable light, Christina looked down at Folly's legs, then frowned.

Out in the yard, Samantha and Christina's dads were leaning against the van, chatting quietly.

"Dad," Christina said unhappily once they were outside. "I think you better take a look at Folly. He seems to be favoring his right foreleg. I was hoping it was just an early-morning crick. But it's lasted all the way out here from the barn."

Her father knelt next to Folly and expertly ran his hands down Folly's leg. He frowned. "Chris, there's a tiny bit of swelling here. Was he at all lame yesterday after your work?"

"No—of course not," Christina said, a worried expression on her face. "I would have mentioned it if he had been. But he was perfectly fine."

Samantha looked at Christina sadly. "Chris, I don't know if Folly can be ridden today."

With a sinking heart, Christina knew that

Samantha was right. So much for her dreams about Newgate. *I guess Ross gets the last laugh this year,* she thought. She swallowed a sigh. Everyone had disappointments, she told herself. Even her mother had had setbacks. Christina knew her mother would want her to take this disappointment in stride and just look ahead to the future. *Sometimes it's really hard, Mom.*

"Well," she said slowly, trying not to show how crushed she was, "let me put Folly away and ask Tor to check him out. Then we should get going so Rebecca doesn't miss dressage today."

Rebecca had been listening to their conversation. "Oh, Chris, I can't believe it!" she cried. "You *have* to compete in Newgate! We've been looking forward to it for months. And I don't want to do it by myself."

"I can't," Christina said in frustration. "There's no way I can risk injuring Folly. Look, we'll just go, as we planned, and watch you compete. That'll be just as much fun," she lied.

Rebecca rolled her eyes. Then her face brightened. "Can't you borrow another horse?"

"How?" Christina said. "I haven't been training with any other horse. I can't just compete on a strange horse, cold." Then her eyes took on a thoughtful look. "Unless . . ." She'd just had an idea. She didn't even know whether to mention it aloud.

"Unless what?" her father prompted.

"Dad—do you think there's any way—" Then

she stopped and shook her head. "I'm crazy for even thinking about it. Never mind. Let me go put Folly away, and we'll hit the road."

"What were you going to say?" Rebecca demanded.

Christina turned back. "Well," she began, slanting a look at Samantha, "I wonder if I could ride Jazz. I've been training with her just as hard as Folly—even harder."

Samantha looked concerned. "She's awfully green."

"Yeah," Christina agreed thoughtfully. "But she's really settled down lately. There's no way we could win today, not after only six months' training. But I'm sure she would be okay—it wouldn't hurt her. And I could still compete. What do you think?" *Please say yes*, Christina thought.

Now that the idea had come to her, she felt a growing excitement. She knew they had enough time to swing by Whitebrook and collect Jazz before heading out on the highway toward Huntington.

Samantha and Christina's dad glanced at each other.

"She *has* been training amazingly well," Samantha said slowly.

"I know she can do it," Christina said. "Please give her—us—a chance."

After a long moment, her dad finally nodded.

"If you want to try it," he said, "it's okay with me.

You and Sammy know what Jazz is capable of."

"Oh, thanks, Dad!" Christina cried, throwing her arms around him. "Thanks! It'll be fine, I know it. It'll be great!" Then, turning, she quickly walked Folly back to his stall.

Tor came over, and she explained how Folly was favoring his right foreleg. Tor promised to look him over, then wished her luck in the show with Jazz. "Be careful," he said, giving her a hug.

"I will. Super-careful," she promised, then turned and ran back to the truck.

Within twenty minutes, Jazz was secured inside the horse trailer next to Marbella, and they were on their way to Huntington.

Two hours later they arrived at the fairgrounds in Huntington, West Virginia. The dressage competition was that afternoon. The following day would be the cross-country and then the show-jumping events. As soon as they had unloaded the horses, Christina checked in with the show organizers. Then she and Rebecca got Marbella and Jazz settled in their temporary stalls.

"His tail looks messy. Do it again."

Christina and Rebecca turned to each other and rolled their eyes when they heard that bossy voice. Craning her head, Christina looked down the stall aisle and saw Ross Townsend giving orders to a young woman. Unlike Christina and Rebecca, who with Kevin's help were braiding their own horses' manes and tails, Ross had one of Townsend Acres' grooms doing the work.

"I guess he's too important to braid his own horse's mane and tail," Christina muttered.

"Yep. Braiding is only for peasants, like us," Rebecca said cheerfully, twisting a bright blue ribbon through Marbella's braid. "Forget about him."

"I'll try," Christina said through gritted teeth.

Later that day, Christina watched Rebecca perform her dressage routine from the area they called "on deck," which was part of the saddling ring. Since Christina was riding right after Rebecca, she was already on Jazz, ready to go. She was studiously ignoring Ross, who was circling Justice in the far corner. Rebecca and Marbella did very well, Christina was glad to see.

As Rebecca rode out of the dressage ring, Christina tightened the strap of her hard hat and prepared to go out. On the far side of the ring, she could see her father and Sammy sitting in the bleachers with their programs and binoculars. Seeing them made Christina feel a little better. As she was about to be called to go into the ring, Ross and Justice sidled up next to her.

"I heard you were trying to retrain a dud flat racer," he sneered. "You must be pretty desperate."

"I have the horse I want," Christina answered coolly, determined not to let him get to her.

"She's got talent, smarts, and heart."

"And she's green as heck," he said. "There's no way you'll do well today."

"I guess we'll find out, won't we?" Christina took a deep, calming breath, then heard her name called. "Excuse me," she said to Ross, false politeness dripping from her voice. "I have a blue ribbon to win." As she turned Jazz to go into the ring, she saw Ross scowling behind her.

Then she was in the ring, touching her finger to her hat in salute to the judges' panel. In truth, she knew she couldn't hope for a blue ribbon today—not on Jazz. The filly was great, but she was just too unschooled. Very few three-year-olds ever competed in three-day eventing; a more experienced and tempered horse was necessary. But Christina would be content with a decent showing and the valuable experience it would give them as a team. *Just do your best, sweetie*, a soothing voice said. *You know what you're doing, and so does Jazz. Concentrate on your filly and trust each other.*

Christina smiled at the sound of the now familiar voice. She straightened her shoulders, took a deep breath, and began.

First move, a measured serpentine to twenty paces, Christina thought, giving Jazz the nearly invisible signal. *Then we'll turn and do a set of left sidesteps, followed by a left leg yield.*

And so their performance began.

*   *   *

"Let's hope you do as well today as you did yesterday," Christina's father told her as she brushed the filly down early the next morning. Today would be the cross-country and show-jumping competition. Christina had done very well in dressage the day before. Jazz had been completely calm and focused in front of the crowds and had moved precisely and elegantly to all of Christina's signals. It had been a terrific first showing.

"Yeah," Christina agreed. "But you know, it was the dressage I was most worried about, since it takes the most training. She's great on cross-country, and I feel pretty confident about the show-jumping, too."

Her father grinned. "I guess you're glad you decided to take a chance on the filly, huh?"

Christina grinned back. "You bet."

Beside her, Rebecca carefully groomed Marbella, then fastened protective wraps around her mare's ankles so she wouldn't tick herself during the jumping. She gave a smothered yawn, then turned to smile sleepily at Christina. They had shared a motel room with Samantha again the night before, and though they had known they should get to bed early, they hadn't been able to resist picking Samantha's brain about the times she had ridden in steeplechases when she was younger.

After the horses were groomed and tacked up,

they heard the bugle call alerting the riders to gather to walk the course. Christina and Rebecca set off together, steadfastly ignoring Ross, who sneered as they passed him. He was in first place so far, after the dressage. Christina was in third. Rebecca was in fifth. But there was a chance of beating him, Christina thought, if she did well in the next two events.

Over the last month, Christina had gradually increased the size of Jazz's jumps at home. Now she saw with relief that the jumps here were only a few inches higher. The filly should be able to leap them with ease, as long as Christina cued her correctly. She and the other riders walked the whole course, memorizing as much as they could and mentally planning how they would best approach each jump.

Then it was time for the competition. Christina was jumping fifth, Rebecca tenth, and Ross fourth. Tensely Christina watched as one rider after another came off the end of the course. Some looked satisfied or pleased, some were frowning and looking upset. Right before Christina's turn Ross rode out of the woods, looking extremely pleased and smug.

Please let me do well, Christina prayed silently. She walked Jazz up to the starting point, then leaned over and whispered in the filly's ear. "Let's just do our best, okay, girl? Just pretend we're at home, riding in the hills in back of Whitebrook. It's just you and me, out having a good time. I love you, girl, and I know we can do it—if we do it together. Now let's get 'em!"

Jazz cocked her ears alertly, seeming to listen to every word Christina said. She whoofed softly and stamped her front leg, as though promising to do her best. Then the whistle was blown, and they were off.

11

THE STARTING POINT WAS AT THE TOP OF A HILL, SO Christina let Jazz canter at her own pace downhill toward the first jump, which was a low stone wall. Silently Christina counted strides and eased Jazz into a collected pace, then gave her the signal at exactly the right moment. *One, two, three, UP*, Christina thought, squeezing her legs. Effortlessly the filly bounded over the wall, seeming to like this new version of the game they played at home.

After the stone wall was a small rise up to a triangular log barrier. They jumped in, then out. On the outward jump Jazz hesitated the slightest bit, but she still leaped over without ticking the log. A water jump followed that, and though water jumps were never Jazz's favorite, Christina urged her through and she took it bravely.

They headed into the woods, cantering down a

narrow dirt path. The sunlight dappled the trail, and the air was still and almost stiflingly hot. Christina felt sweat trickle down the side of her face.

After a wide turn they encountered a rustic parallel jump, two thick logs resting on top of each other. Gleefully Jazz flew over them without a hitch, then cantered down the trail. Christina kept the reins gathered, slowing the filly a bit. Speed counted, and riders could be penalized for going under the optimum time.

As they came out of the woods and headed toward the last three obstacles, Christina allowed herself a split second of satisfaction. Jazz Goddess was jumping with interest and enthusiasm and yet was alert to Christina's every command, and instantly responsive. She was putting in a terrific performance, a performance worthy of a much older and more seasoned animal. Once again Christina felt a rush of love for the beautiful black filly whom she had raised from birth. They were soul sisters.

The final three obstacles were a tall embankment, a wide ditch with a low hedge, and a coop—a small building slanted like the roof of a chicken coop. Without hesitation Jazz bounded over each one, her powerful hindquarters springing them into the air.

After the last jump Christina let the filly out into a well-paced gallop, and Jazz surged toward the

161

finish line. Then Christina slowed Jazz, first to a canter, then a trot, cooling the filly down. She had no real idea of their time, but she believed they had scored well on the jumps. When she circled around to the saddling ring where she would dismount, she was surprised to see Samantha and Rebecca grinning and jumping up and down.

"You've got the best time so far!" Samantha cried, holding Jazz's bridle so Christina could dismount.

"I do?" Christina asked in amazement. "Incredible!" She threw her arms around Jazz's neck and kissed her.

"If you do well this afternoon, you just might get a ribbon," Rebecca said happily.

Christina was thrilled. She really hadn't been expecting to do well at this meet. But Jazz was coming through for her, doing her best. Happy tears floated in her eyes as she walked the filly around, cooling her down. "I always knew we'd be a great team, Jazz," she said softly as the filly stopped for a mouthful of grass. "And I think my mom knew it too. You're really something special."

Jazz raised her head momentarily to whoof softly and nibble Christina's shoulder, tickling her.

The Whitebrook crowd ate a picnic lunch under the deep shade of a maple tree in the field behind the fairgrounds. Marbella and Jazz were tied nearby, and they were grazing lightly in the shade.

Rebecca was in sixth place overall, and to her shock, Christina was tied for second with Ross. She could feel her stomach knotting in anticipation of the show-jumping that afternoon.

But when the time came to mount up and ride on deck, waiting for her turn, a sense of calm came over Christina. It really didn't matter if she won, or even if Ross beat her. She was doing what she loved, what she was born to do, on a horse that meant more to her than anything in the world. She really couldn't ask for more than that. Her mother would understand how she felt, Christina was sure. Leaning down, she patted Jazz's neck. "Let's do it, girl," she said, walking her up to the ring.

She thought about the look Ross had given her as he passed her to take his turn. He had glared at her, an ugly expression marring his face. He had been as shocked as she was to see they were tied, and earlier Christina had seen him arguing with his mother. His mom seemed to be urging him to win no matter what. Christina had been more thankful than ever that her father supported her but didn't pressure her. She was glad Mrs. Townsend wasn't her mother.

But now Ross was riding off the course, a smug, self-satisfied look on his face. He had jumped clean, the first rider to do so. Giving Christina a gloating look, he greeted his mother, who was waiting for him. His father was also nearby but was talking on a cellular phone and could manage only a small wave at his son. But Lavinia hugged Ross proudly and kissed his cheek.

Then Christina was called, and she trotted out to salute the judges. Her mind went on automatic pilot as she instinctively urged Jazz into a canter toward the first jump. These jumps required more mental concentration and planning than those on the cross-country course. She had already walked the course and planned her strategy, and now she followed her plan, counting strides, giving the filly the correct aids. Every ounce of concentration and focus she had was centered on the filly and the jumps coming up.

One after another they cleared a parallel, a brush jump, an oxer, a large spread . . . and they were jumping cleanly, and in decent time, Christina knew. It would be so amazing if they managed to place . . .

Using all her years of experience in jumping, Christina focused on Jazz, giving her the signals she needed to help her get over the obstacles. Although the filly was green, Christina's knowledge was helping to make up for it.

As they approached the last jump, a two-fence combination, Christina started counting strides. They were almost home free. Even if they ticked this last fence, they would still be in great shape. To her right, Christina was only dimly aware of the silent crowd of spectators sitting in the bleachers outside of the ring.

Four more big strides. Okay, Jazz, this is it, girl. . . . Then suddenly a burst of bright color sailed into Christina's line of vision. It was a ladies' wide-brimmed hat, in bright cherry red. The wind must have taken it, and now it tumbled directly in front of them, almost brushing Jazz's nose.

Jazz snorted in fear, and before Christina could collect her wits or the reins the horse burst forward in a gallop straight toward the last fence. Christina immediately hauled back on the reins, but the large, powerful Thoroughbred was clearly terrified and couldn't be stopped.

No! Christina thought, watching the fence rush toward them with sickening speed. *We can never make it! Not going this fast!* "Whoa, Jazz!" she yelled fiercely, determined to protect the filly from disaster. Using all her strength, she pulled hard on the reins, leaning back with her body. "Whoa, Jazz! Stop, girl, stop!"

But Jazz was already at the foot of the jump. The filly made a gallant effort to get over it, but they were in too close. Christina felt Jazz's hind feet catch hard on the fence, then the ground was rushing up to meet her. Jazz's front legs crumpled beneath them, and they were going down.

Every instinct kicked in as Christina automatically loosened the stirrups from her boots and tried to jump away from Jazz, who was flailing and falling. But it was too late, and she was trapped as Jazz

165

toppled over her. Christina's last sight was of Jazz's beautiful black coat, slick with sweat, falling right down on top of her. *I'm going to die. Mom, oh Mom, please help me.* Then a crushing weight came down on Christina, and dust and horse hair were in her nose and mouth, and everything went dark.

"Honey? Sweetie, can you hear me? It's Daddy."

Daddy? I haven't called him that since I was a little girl. Christina tried to open her eyes, but she was so sleepy that she just couldn't manage it.

"Chris? Can you say anything? It's Sammy."

What's Sammy doing in my bedroom? Christina wondered. *Why is everyone being so weird?* With a great effort, she tried again to open her eyes. Something felt wrong with her face—it was puffy and stiff. But she finally managed to open one eye. As soon as she did that, she was conscious of extreme pain, all over her body. She groaned.

Her dad took her hand, and she tried to squeeze it, but her fingers hurt.

"Dad—where am I?" she whispered. Her lips felt dry and cracked.

"Oh, honey, it's good to hear your voice," her father said, smiling down at her. "God, we've been so worried about you."

"What happened? Where's Jazz? Is she okay?"

"Yes, sweetie, Jazz is okay, miraculously enough," Samantha answered soothingly. "But you guys took quite a tumble. Do you remember the jump yesterday?"

Then it all came back to her—the image of that bright, cheerful hat, Jazz spooking, unstoppable, the fence . . .

Christina moaned a little. "I feel like I got hit by a truck," she admitted. "Are you sure Jazz is okay?"

"She pulled a tendon—nothing more. She'll be fine. But, honey, we need to talk about you. You're in the hospital."

At her father's suddenly serious tone, Christina frowned, or tried to. It hurt too much, so she gave it up. Managing to pry the other eye open, she glanced down at her body. Her left leg was in a cast from her foot to her hip. Her ribs were bandaged, and even without touching them she could tell they were extremely tender. Her right hand was also in a small cast.

"Oh, no," she muttered. "What a mess. How bad is it? How long till I can ride again?"

She was aware of her dad and Samantha sending each other looks.

"Honey," her father began, "you had a really bad fall. Let's just take it easy and get better, and worry about riding later."

Slowly, Christina said, "What's wrong? Tell me what's wrong."

Samantha answered gently. "Well, you banged yourself up pretty good. You cracked a couple ribs,

167

sprained your right wrist really badly, and bruised a couple of other bones—like your jawbone." She forced a grin. "You also have two black eyes, which makes you look kind of like a blond raccoon."

Christina didn't smile back.

"Thank heavens you didn't fracture your skull— or worse," Samantha said quietly. "Your hard hat protected you."

"What about my leg?" Christina asked. "What's wrong with it?"

Her father stroked her shoulder through the starchy hospital sheet. "You broke your shinbone," he told her.

Christina felt relieved. "Okay, so I'll wear a cast, and then maybe by December or January, I can ride again, right?"

Her father and Samantha were silent.

"Just *tell* me!" Christina cried, then immediately regretted it as pain shot through her body. She stifled a gasp and tried to lie very still, her eyes closed.

"Christina—when Jazz fell, she pinned your left leg beneath her for just a second," her father explained reluctantly. "It put your knee under a lot of stress and, well . . ."

"Honey, what your dad means is, your knee was crushed," Samantha said, blinking hard. "You had surgery last night."

Christina opened her eyes and looked at Samantha. She felt the blood draining out of her face. Suddenly she felt incredibly exhausted, and pain was throbbing throughout her body. "Surgery?" she murmured. She had no recollection of it at all.

"There were bone fragments to be cleaned out. And they had to reattach some of your muscles. Actually, you don't have a kneecap anymore."

Christina's eyes widened. "What are you saying?" she whispered. She saw Samantha swallow and look at Mr. Reese.

He cleared his throat. "Right now you're in a cast, but in a month or two you'll need another operation. Actually, the doctor said . . ." His voice faltered. "He said you'll probably need at least three more operations over the next couple of years. Right now you have pins holding your leg straight, but those have to come out. They're going to put in an artificial knee joint." He smiled very weakly. "A Teflon one. You'll be the bionic woman."

"I don't understand," Christina said softly. "When will I be able to ride?"

"Honey, what we're trying to say is that it's going to be a very long time before you'll be able to ride," her father said, his mouth a tight line. "The doctor said possibly in a couple of years, but— Chris, I hate to tell you this, but you may not be able to ride again. Your knee just won't work the way it always did. I'm sorry, sweetie. I'm so sorry. But I'm glad you're alive."

169

Christina stared at him in shock, her hazel eyes, so like her mother's, staring into his warm blue ones. For a moment the room seemed to swim around her. All she could see was her father's face, lined with pain, and the glowing white walls of the hospital room.

"Not ride?" she repeated, feeling stupid. "Not ride again? Not ride Jazz anymore?"

Samantha leaned over and brushed Christina's blond bangs gently off her bruised and scraped forehead. "Try not to think about it right now. Let's just take it one day at a time, okay? Right now you have to get better so we can move you back to Lexington. Guess who's driving up to see you? Tor. He's bringing you a special present."

"I don't want it," Christina said thickly.

"Grandma and Grandpa Griffen came up last night," her dad said. "And Rebecca and Kevin are here, just outside. They can't wait to see you—they've been so worried."

"I don't want to see them."

"I have an idea," Samantha said with forced brightness. "Why don't I go downstairs to the cafeteria and see if I can rustle you up a nice hot-fudge sundae. I bet that would help."

Christina glared at her. "Sammy, don't you get it? I might not be able to ride again—ever again! It's all I've ever dreamed about—all I ever worked for. For three years I've been raising Jazz, dreaming about riding her, competing on her." Hot tears began to sting her eyes, but she didn't stop. "I wanted to go to the Olympics one day! I wanted to ride Jazz in the Olympics! Now I'm only thirteen years old, and my career is over, finished. Don't you understand? Oh, God!" She was crying in earnest now and brought up her hand to rub her eyes. The cast on her right wrist bonked her bruised forehead and she grimaced. Her wracking sobs made it feel like hot pokers were being pushed through her cracked ribs, but she couldn't stop.

Soon she was aware of the brush of cold alcohol on the side of her arm and then the icy, stinging prick of a needle. Minutes later, her sobs quieted and slowed, and then she drifted off into a drugged, heavy sleep.

Much later that evening, Christina awoke. Her hospital room was dark, with the only light coming from the streetlamp outside. Once her eyes adjusted, she could see her father slouched in the room's easy chair, asleep. He must be very uncomfortable, she thought.

Her eyes still felt puffy and thick, and she could feel the scratchy, stiff threads of stitches inside her mouth. She hadn't noticed them before. Everything still ached, and her leg in particular felt heavy with pain. Christina lay very still. On a small rolling table to one side, she could see her dinner, cold now and congealed. She wasn't hungry anyway.

She thought about Jazz and wondered where she was, if she had been vanned back to Whitebrook. Suddenly Christina's heart ached with an unbearable need to see the filly, to make sure she was okay, to hug her and kiss her. Her fingers twitched inside their cast as she imagined stroking the thick, silky black coat, touching the velvety nose. She imagined Jazz looking at her, her large, liquid brown eyes blinking intelligently, sending her messages of love and devotion.

Oh, Jazz. I'm so sorry, girl. But it wasn't our fault. I hope they ban hats at these meets from now on. I can't wait to see you, girl, to hold you. Everything will be okay as soon as I can see you.

Christina turned her head and looked across the room at her sleeping father. She felt a twinge of guilt as she remembered the terrible things she had said, how mean she had been, when all he and Samantha wanted to do was help her. Swallowing back a lump in her throat, she resolved to apologize to everyone tomorrow.

But what was she going to do with herself? What would her life be like if she couldn't ever ride again, couldn't ever feel the joy of the wind on her face as she thundered down the trails at Whitebrook? And competing—she loved it. There was nothing more exciting than pitting herself against other riders, other horses.

Her leg began throbbing painfully. It felt as though a huge, white-hot pair of hands was squeezing it, twisting her knee. Christina bit her lip. Her ribs ached more now too, probably because she had been crying. Maybe she should wake her dad, ask for help. But he was sleeping so heavily, and she thought he probably hadn't gotten much sleep the night before.

Then, as she lay there, tears of pain trickling down her cheeks, the door opened silently. A white-garbed nurse came in quietly and smiled hello. Christina couldn't smile back. With a sympathetic look, the nurse carefully took her temperature and noted it on her chart. Then she took Christina's blood pressure, which hurt since her arm muscles were still horribly sore.

"Are you in a lot of pain, dear?" the nurse asked softly, leaning over the bed.

Wordlessly, Christina managed to nod.

"I can give you one more pain shot tonight," the nurse said. "Just a second." Once again Christina felt the swab of alcohol on the side of her arm, then the prick of a needle. With a final smile and reassuring pat, the nurse left as silently as she had come.

The pain medicine worked very quickly. With a grateful smile of relief, Christina felt the throbbing in her leg ease to a dull ache. Her ribs felt better, as did her wrist. *Thank heavens*, she thought.

Sweetheart? Are you okay? I was so worried.

Christina looked around groggily, but there was no one in her room except her father. A comforting warmth stole over her, and she nestled back into her pillow, feeling much better. *Mom.*

I know it's been rough, but it'll get better, you'll see. There's still so much for you to do.

It was very hard for Christina to keep her eyes open now. She felt deliciously comfortable and sleepy. The voice she was imagining was so soothing, so full of love.

You know, even if you don't ride again, there's a lot you can accomplish. You can still train horses, or be a vet, or even be a breeding manager. You can't give up, sweetie, not now. Besides, Jazz needs you. You need to take care of her. Promise me you won't give up. Promise me you'll trust yourself. Do you hear me, Christina? Promise me that.

Groggily Christina felt herself slipping off into blessed sleep, but before she did, she mumbled, "I promise. I promise, Mom. I won't let you down."

Part Three

12

ON CHRISTMAS DAY TWO MONTHS BEFORE, CHRISTINA had turned sixteen. It had been a long three years since her terrible accident. She hadn't ridden at all for eighteen months—her time had been taken up with operations and physical therapy. She had missed a great deal of school and had tutors at home for the first eight months.

But her determination had won out, and she was in the saddle again.

"Easy on your approach," Tor called to Christina as she headed Jazz Goddess toward a five-foot oxer.

Christina nodded to show she had heard, then squeezed with her legs to give Jazz the signal. As usual the sleek black Thoroughbred sailed easily over the tall obstacle, landing neatly on the other side. Grinning, Christina turned the mare and headed back to where Tor was waiting, his cheeks pink in the nippy February air.

Her knee ached. After having an artificial knee joint put in, she had plunged into physical therapy, strengthening the torn muscles and learning how to walk all over again. From a wheelchair, she had quickly graduated to crutches, then a walker, then a sturdy cane. She had made terrific progress and soon was working hard to eliminate any trace of a limp. Sheer determination kept her striving to achieve her goal: to ride again.

However, once she could walk well, she found that didn't automatically mean she could ride. When she sat on a horse, her knee was bent in an unnatural position. For most people, this presented no problem; their joints had the flexibility and strength to make the adjustment. But for Christina, it was a disaster. Her new knee joint bent only one way, and it was pretty rigid. The muscles had been torn and repaired but were still weak. The first time Christina tentatively swung a leg over Jazz's back, then lowered herself into the saddle, she had gasped with pain and tears had come to her eyes. But she had practiced night after night in the barn when no one was around to hear her groan with pain. Slowly, slowly she had stretched her damaged muscles until they could accommodate the new, unnatural position. Then she had begun riding again in earnest.

Tor smiled as he took Jazz's bridle so Christina

could dismount. "Nice," he said approvingly. "No wonder you two have become the stars of the three-day circuit."

Christina swung her right leg over the back of the saddle, then slowly eased herself to the ground, letting her arms control her weight. After eighteen months of riding, she no longer winced when she dismounted.

But she knew later that night her knee would be swollen and throbbing with pain. She would rub it with liniment, then wrap it with an Ace bandage as she always did. Many people would have given up long before now and simply accepted that there were some things they couldn't do after sustaining this kind of injury. But not Christina. During her darkest moments, when she was weeping with pain in her room, trying to be quiet so her father wouldn't hear, she remembered the voice she had heard. In the hospital the voice had asked her to promise not to give up, and she had given her word. Now, no matter what, she knew she couldn't go back on that promise. It kept her going when everything inside her screamed to stop, to give up, to let it rest.

She walked Jazz around the Whitebrook stable yard, moving slowly, concentrating on not letting her knee buckle with fatigue. When they were both cooled out, she led the mare into the barn for grooming. Tor had gone back to his stable to teach a late-afternoon class.

It was a relief to get inside the warm, comforting barn on this chilly winter day, overcast and damp. Her knee ached more on days like this. Gritting her teeth, Christina put Jazz in crossties and got out her grooming equipment.

"Hey—why don't you sit a minute and I'll do that," Kevin McLean offered, coming down the main aisle of the training barn.

For a moment Christina was tempted. As she was about to refuse out of pride, Kevin gently took the body brush out of her hand and pointed to a nearby hay bale. Christina sighed and sat down on the bale, absently rubbing her knee.

"Thanks," she said. "Maybe I overdid it a little today."

Kevin didn't even look up. Although he was a few months younger than Christina and wouldn't turn sixteen until May, he was already several inches taller. His red hair had darkened to a deep auburn color, and his freckles were hidden by his permanently browned skin. In the long months when Christina couldn't ride, he, along with Rebecca, Samantha, and Tor, had kept Jazz in perfect shape. Kevin had been the one to take her for long cross-country rides to maintain her stamina and muscle tone. Rebecca and Samantha had kept up with her jumping and dressage training under Tor's watchful eye. Christina had spent many an hour, her leg in a cast or a brace, propped up on a stool outside the training ring, watching her beloved mare go through her paces. As a result Jazz hadn't lost any time in her training and now, three years later, was exceptionally well schooled, despite her young age.

"You always overdo it," Kevin said evenly, brushing every last bit of winter mud out of Jazz's gleaming black coat.

Christina laughed. "I guess I do."

Her father came out of his office. "Hi, sweetie," he said, kissing the top of Christina's head. "How was your lesson?"

As soon as he had walked over, Christina had sat up straight and quit rubbing her knee. She knew he still worried about her, and she was determined not to add to his tension.

"It was good. Sometimes it seems like Jazz can jump anything. Whatever we throw at her, she just seems to think it's a game."

In her crossties, Jazz whickered and bobbed her head a bit.

They laughed, and Kevin playfully patted Jazz's rump. "Show-off," he said.

Her father lowered himself next to Christina on the hay bale and stretched out his long legs. One of Delaney's latest offspring, a brown tabby named Nutmeg, came up and began to twine around Mr. Reese's ankles.

"No wonder you guys did so well last year," her

father said. Christina and Jazz, in their first year back competing, had been very successful. During the fall shows they'd won quite a few blue ribbons, building up their total points score so they could qualify for some of the biggest and most prestigious meets.

"It was really Jazz," Christina said modestly. "Everyone kept her in such good shape, all I had to do was get on her."

"Uh-huh." Her dad looked over at Kevin, who was using a polishing cloth on the mare. "So what are your plans for this year?"

Christina looked at him in surprise. It was only the beginning of February; she wouldn't start competing until next month. Usually she, Samantha, and Tor decided what shows she would enter, and although she always checked with her father first, he never questioned her plans or what she was doing.

She thought she might know where her dad was heading with this. Last year, she had been so determined to make up for eighteen months' absence that she had competed as much as she possibly could. The end result was that she had overstressed her knee badly and had to wear her brace again for a while; her school grades had gone down, so she'd had to get extra tutoring for algebra and chemistry; and even Jazz had started seeming bored with the constant drill of training and competing. Also, Christina had ended up having to dip into her trust fund for some of the entry fees, which her dad hadn't been too thrilled about.

"This year I'm going to enter only the most important shows," Christina said casually, trying to sound thoughtful and reasonable. "There's Fair Hill in Maryland, Groton in Connecticut, Briarsley in Danville . . . and a couple of local hunt club shows, like Kentucky Riders and Blucher Farms." She slanted a glance at her dad to see his reaction.

"Uh-huh. Cut to the chase. How many shows total?" he said dryly.

"Um . . . nineteen," she said in a very low voice.

"Make it eight, tops," her father said firmly.

"Dad!" Christina turned wide hazel eyes on him. "Only eight? I can't. I need more shows to build up my points to qualify for the major meets." She sat up straight to look at him pleadingly. Over the last three years she had finally let her blond hair grow out, and it now was below her shoulders. Like Samantha, she usually wore it in a tidy French braid.

For a moment her father didn't respond. "Honey, I think your health is more important than qualifying for the major shows," he said finally, not looking at her.

"My knee is fine," Christina insisted. "And I'll keep my grades up—no tutors, no summer school. That way I'll have plenty of time to go to the summer meets."

"Ten," he relented. "But nothing else. No teaching

182

classes at Tor and Sammy's, no extra groom work, no exercise riding for me, no training other horses. Are we clear? You overdid it so much last year that you almost had to have another operation to repair your muscles. I won't go through that again."

When her father spoke so firmly, Christina knew he meant business. But it seemed so unfair! She loved exercise-riding her father's Thoroughbreds as they pounded around the track like lightning. And training other horses kept her on her toes and gave her valuable experience. And she would be heartbroken to give up her beginning riders class of five- and six-year-olds at the Nelsons'. Giving her father a sideways glance, Christina could see the determined set of his chin. She sighed, but the battle wasn't over yet.

"Fourteen," she said briskly. "Otherwise there'll be no way to have the points I need."

"Twelve. And that's my final offer," her dad said in a tone that brooked no argument. "What do you need all these points for, anyway? You know you'll get into Groton easily."

Christina bit her lip. She hadn't planned on telling her father so soon; she was afraid he wouldn't let her go ahead with her plan. Kevin was busily picking Jazz's feet, pretending he wasn't listening to every word. Frowning, Christina muttered, "The Rolex Kentucky."

Kevin stopped and looked up in surprise, still

holding Jazz's foot. Next to Christina, Mr. Reese straightened and stared at her.

"That's the biggest show in America," he said. "One of the most important in the world. Olympic-class riders compete there."

Leaning over, Christina brushed some dirt off her breeches. "I know," she said in a little voice. But her chin was set firmly. Years before, as she had lain in her hospital bed, staring with horror at the eight-inch scar running down her knee, she had decided that she wasn't going to let it stop her. She was going to the top of her profession—she was going to be one of the best, just like her mother before her. Doing well at the Rolex Kentucky was the way to get there.

"Do you think Jazz is up to it?" her father asked.

"I do."

"Do you think you're up to it?"

"I'm going to do my best," Christina said.

"Hmm." Her father sat there silently for a few minutes, while Christina waited anxiously to see if she had to come up with more ammo. Finally he stood and brushed hay off his jeans, then leaned over and smoothed her hair. "Twelve meets, and no more. Rolex Kentucky if the doctor says okay *after* the twelfth show. Deal?"

Christina knew it was the best offer she'd get. "Deal."

Her dad headed back to the office, while Christina

184

marveled at the fact that he hadn't forbidden her to aim that high. Grinning at Kevin, she punched her fist in the air. "Yes!"

Taking Jazz out of the crossties, Kevin shook his head. "I hope you know what you're doing."

Christina got up to walk Jazz down to her stall. "I do, I'm sure of it. Thanks for grooming her."

"No prob." Kevin opened the mare's stall door, and Jazz went in agreeably. Together Christina and Kevin gave her fresh water and filled her hay net, then measured out her evening portion of grain and concentrated feed.

"Oh, I wanted to ask you something," Kevin said with studied casualness as he poured oats into Jazz's feed bucket. "The Valentine's Dance is coming up at school. I was wondering . . . if you want to go together."

Christina smiled. "Sure. We can just hang out, and that way we won't have to worry about getting actual dates."

Rolling his eyes, Kevin gave an exaggerated sigh. "No. You don't get it. *I* am asking *you* on an *actual* date. To the Valentine's Dance."

Suddenly Christina's brain ceased working. She and Kevin had lived next door to each other their whole lives. For heaven's sake, when they were in kindergarten they used to sleep over at each other's houses! She had a picture of them taking a bath together when they were toddlers! A deep-crimson blush washed up her neck and face to her forehead. They had always been best pals, like brother and sister. Now he was asking her out . . .

With a rueful smile, Kevin shook his head. "Never mind," he said kindly. "Forget I mentioned it. We don't have to go."

"No!" Christina blurted. "I mean . . . that is . . . I'd like to go with you. To the dance, I mean," she babbled.

A real smile lit Kevin's face. "Great," he said. "We'll work out the plan later. I better be getting home for dinner."

"Me too," Christina said faintly as they headed down the aisle. She was excruciatingly conscious of Kevin walking beside her. For once her knee wasn't bothering her after her ride—her mind was whirling with surprise instead of pain.

They parted at the end of the stable yard, and Kevin went to the McLeans' cottage while she headed to the farmhouse. Inside, she went up to her room to shower before dinner. She still couldn't believe that Kevin had asked her on a *date*. She just didn't think of him that way, although she had heard girls at school gossiping about him. Kevin, cute?

Frowning, she stepped out of the shower and wrapped herself in a towel. As she started to untangle her hair, she thought about the dance and what it would be like. She decided it would be okay. For her part, she would just go with Kevin and treat him as she always had, and play it by ear.

As she quickly dressed in jeans and a sweater, she wished she had someone to talk to about it. Of course, she would tell Rebecca right away. But Rebecca couldn't really give motherly *advice*. And Samantha, though Christina totally adored her and trusted her, was Kevin's sister. *Mom, I might be sixteen, but I need you more than ever.*

13

"YOU'RE KIDDING ME," REBECCA SAID THE NEXT DAY AS they were saddling their horses at the Nelsons' stable. Christina had just told her best friend about Kevin's surprising invitation.

"Uh-uh," Christina confirmed, tightening the girth strap on her borrowed bay mare. Since Jazz was at Whitebrook, Samantha and Tor allowed Christina to use one of their stable horses for class. "It's a real date."

"Wow." Rebecca digested this information. "Well, it's about time you noticed what a great guy he is."

"I know he's a great guy. I just never thought of him as a boyfriend," Christina admitted. "He's always been like my brother. I mean, we grew up living on the same farm. Now all of a sudden, I'm starting to look at him a little differently, you know?"

Rebecca nodded, then lowered her stirrup irons. She turned to grin at Christina. "I hope you two have a great time. I'm going with—"

"Kyle Parrish!" Christina supplied, laughing. Rebecca's dreams had come true when she and the good-looking junior had started dating earlier in the school year.

Tor came into the ring, looking professional in his breeches, white turtleneck, and dark-blue riding jacket. He clapped his hands.

"Okay, class, let's mount up. I want to take you over some wide rustics today. We're going to be sharpening our advanced-jumping skills, getting ready for the spring trials. Which reminds me— Chris, I need your entry fee for Fair Hill by the end of the week." Fair Hill in Maryland was the first of the bigger shows that she would be competing in. It was held at the very beginning of March.

"Okay." Christina nodded, then led her mare over to a mounting step near the door. Since her accident, she could no longer put her left foot in its stirrup and bounce up into the saddle. Even a leg up didn't really help—it put too much stress on her knee. So she climbed up on the mounting step, like a little kid, and slid over into her saddle.

"Now, let's warm up," Tor said, striding to the center of the ring.

In this advanced class there were only four students, and Christina and Rebecca were the youngest ones. The others, a man and a woman, were both in their early twenties and had been competing for several years.

Christina took her mare around the large indoor training ring at a trot and then a canter. Then, when the first student finished the course, she headed for the first jump, a huge solid fence painted to look like a stone wall. It was four feet, ten inches tall and almost as wide. Even so, it wasn't as big as some of the fences she'd be facing later this spring and summer.

Automatically Christina counted strides, then squeezed with her legs at exactly the right moment. Her horse sprang with powerful hindquarters and effortlessly jumped over the fence, landing squarely on the other side. Christina immediately looked ahead to the next jump and turned her mount toward the middle of the ring, where a rough log triangle had been set up. Horse and rider leaped in, then quickly out again, and circled the ring once more.

"Good!" Tor called. "Chris, work on keeping her a little more collected. She has a tendency to rush at the jump. Good jump, though."

The lesson continued. From the very first jump, Christina's knee had begun to ache, but she put it out of her mind. Through the years of rehabilitation, Christina had worked hard with Beth McLean to develop new ways of moving and riding that put less stress on her knee. But it still hurt to do the thing she loved most in the world.

"Now let's try the spread jump," Tor instructed, pointing to the left.

Christina turned the mare and followed Tor's motions. Again and again they jumped over the large obstacles as she concentrated on keeping perfect form before, during, and after the jumps.

"Excellent, Chris! Well done," Tor said.

Christina blushed at the praise. By the time the lesson was over, it was dark outside and she was exhausted with the strain of keeping her leg in the proper position. When she dismounted, her left leg almost buckled, and she buried her face against her mare's warm side so the others wouldn't see the pain on her face. Then she took a deep breath and slowly led her horse toward the stable for cooling out.

"Hi, sweetie," Samantha said, popping her head out of her office. "Everything okay?"

Christina knew she meant, "How is your knee?"

"Fine," Christina said firmly. "What about you?" Pointedly she looked at Samantha's maternity smock. No one had been more delighted than Christina when Samantha and Tor had announced they were expecting a baby in late April.

"Fine, fine," Samantha said, walking with Christina down the aisle toward the mare's stall. "I'm always hot, though. It's like having a built-in furnace."

"Have you guys started your Lamaze classes?" Christina loved hearing about all the details of Samantha's pregnancy. She'd been hoping for a long time that her favorite couple would have a baby.

Samantha giggled, then lowered herself awkwardly to a bench while Christina began to groom the bay mare. "We had our first class last night. They showed us a movie of an actual birth, and I thought Tor was going to faint. Later I pointed out that he had seen a million foals be born, but he insisted it was different somehow." Grinning, Samantha rubbed her lower back.

Christina chuckled. She was already planning the baby shower she was going to have for Samantha and Tor. She would have to enlist Beth and Rebecca's help.

Once Christina was back at home she did her evening chores, which these days consisted mostly of taking care of Jazz.

"Hey, girl," Christina crooned as she quickly pitched soiled straw out of the stall. "I wish I could have spent the day with you instead of going to school and taking that dumb history quiz."

Jazz whoofed and affectionately nibbled the back of Christina's jacket.

Christina pretended Jazz was making conversation. "Yeah, I know. I think I did okay, though. Don't worry—I'll make good grades this semester."

After the stall was clean and fresh straw was spread on its floor, Christina filled Jazz's hay net and gave her her evening grain. Then, feeling a bone-deep weariness and an aching pain in her knee that seemed to shoot straight up into her hip, Christina made her way back to the farmhouse.

Minutes later she was gingerly sinking into bathwater as hot as she could stand it. Later she would put an ice pack on her knee. As she slowly leaned back against the tub, tears of pain squeezed out from beneath her lashes. Sometimes she just didn't know how much she could take. Being in almost constant pain was so wearing, so discouraging. And she knew she only made it worse on herself by her insistence on riding. But what could she do? Quitting now would be like cutting off a limb, or losing her sight. Her life would be bland, colorless without Jazz, without competing. She had to go on. But sometimes she just didn't know how she could.

"Oh, God, I don't know about this," Christina muttered, staring at the tube Beth McLean was holding out. They were in the upstairs bathroom at the farmhouse, and Beth and Samantha were both helping Christina and Rebecca get ready for the Valentine's Dance.

From where she was perched on the edge of the tub, Samantha smirked, and Beth shot her a dark look. Then she turned back to Christina. "It isn't a *snake*, Chris," she said with exaggerated patience. "It's mascara. Now come on, open your eyes wide."

Rebecca was already at the mirror, competently brushing blush across her cheeks. Her short, brown curly hair held tiny sprigs of baby's breath, and her dress was a pale rose color.

"It makes my eyelids heavy," Christina complained when the mascara had been applied. She peered into the mirror. "But I guess it does make my eyes look bigger," she admitted.

"See, I knew you would like it. Now let me do something with your hair."

"Thank heavens Beth was there to help me when I was getting ready for my wedding," Samantha said, reaching over her large stomach to plug in the curling iron. "Otherwise I would have had to get married with a hard hat on my head."

Christina couldn't help giggling.

At eight o'clock, the doorbell rang. Kyle and Kevin were waiting on the doorstep, small plastic boxes in their hands.

Hesitantly Christina came down the stairs. For the last sixteen years, she had never felt the slightest bit of self-consciousness in front of Kevin. He had seen her covered with mud, sweaty and dirty, with horse droppings clinging to her boots; he'd seen her through some truly awful haircuts, through poison ivy and chicken pox. And of course, he'd seen her crying with pain, her knee bruised and swollen from the latest operation, her long scar held together with metal staples, ribbons of yellow and green radiating out from it. He had always been right there in the hospital, helping her into a wheelchair, rolling her IV stand alongside.

Now, all of a sudden, Christina felt uncharacteristically shy and ill at ease. Her long blond hair had been curled and gathered on top of her head, with long tendrils hanging down to frame her face. She was wearing makeup, which made her feel weird, but also, she knew, enhanced her natural good looks. Her dress, purchased on advice of Rebecca, was long and floaty, in a muted sage green that made her hazel eyes stand out.

Kevin was waiting at the bottom of the stairs. His green eyes widened when he saw her, and a slow smile spread across his face. He looked tall and handsome in his dark suit. Christina smiled when she saw his tie had small horses all over it.

"These are for you," Kevin said, and handed her a corsage of small pink rosebuds.

From there the evening just got better and better. Kyle had borrowed his mother's car, and Christina was glad they didn't have to go in a pickup truck.

At school they entered the large gym, which had been decorated with large paper hearts, red and white streamers, and red, pink, and white balloons. Usually Christina hated sappy stuff like that, but

195

tonight she found the effect magical. A local band was playing hits from the sixties all the way to the nineties. Because of her knee, Christina had to sit out a lot of the dances, but Kevin didn't seem to mind.

"So, are you enjoying your first high school dance?" he asked her at one point, handing her a glass of punch. Because of the accident, she had missed all the social events of her freshman and sophomore years.

"I like it," she said with surprise. "I didn't know if I would, but I do. I'm having fun. It's great to see everyone all dressed up—they look so different."

Later they danced several slow dances, and Christina marveled at how it felt to be in Kevin's arms—a little strange, but also nice. He was familiar, comforting, and yet this was all so new. Tonight their relationship was moving in a new direction, and though it was scary, it also felt right somehow.

Around eleven o'clock, the four friends decided to go to a coffee bar in Lexington before heading home. Once they were in a booth with their hot drinks in front of them, Kyle said, "That was a great dance. The spring prom is going to be a lot of fun too. I hear they're going to have a Hawaiian theme."

Christina laughed. "Kyle, that's months away. I can't even think about it yet."

"That's funny," Kevin said. "The Rolex Kentucky

isn't until mid-May, but you have *that* all figured out."

"That's different," Christina protested as the others laughed.

"Whew—the Rolex. That's a serious meet," Kyle said. "Next stop, the Olympics."

"I'm just going to do my best," Christina said, playing with her straw. "I know Jazz can handle it."

"Ross Townsend is talking about it too," Kyle said. Kyle's older sister took lessons from the same teacher as Ross—an ex–Olympic champion. "He seems pretty determined. My sister says he's obsessed."

Christina frowned. The year before, when she had been competing aggressively, she and Ross had had a lot of showdowns. She had ended up winning more than he had, and he hadn't taken it well. "Ross should get a life," she said.

"I heard his parents separated for a little while, then got back together," Rebecca said.

"Oh, let's not gossip about them," Christina pleaded. "Why ruin such a great night?"

All too soon, it was time for them to head home. Kyle and Rebecca dropped Christina and Kevin off at Whitebrook. Slowly Christina and Kevin walked down the gravel drive toward the McLeans' cottage and the farmhouse. At the Reeses' door, Christina stopped, suddenly feeling awkward again. But Kevin smiled his same old smile and tugged on one of her curls, and she instantly felt better.

"Thanks for going with me," he said. "I had a great time."

"Me too."

"Does that mean that maybe you'd like to go on an actual date again?"

Christina smiled up at him. "Yeah. If you can catch me when I'm not completely worn out from training. Things are going to start heating up now for the spring trials."

"Okay. I'll be on the lookout." Then Kevin lowered his head to hers and gently kissed her.

Christina's eyes flew open, then fluttered shut as a tingle went down her spine. She kissed him back, experimentally, deciding she liked it. Then they said good night, and she let herself into the farmhouse. Humming, she made her way upstairs, not caring one bit that it was after midnight and she would have to get up in less than five hours to work Jazz.

14

"YO, CRIP."

Involuntarily Christina's neck muscles tightened at the sardonic voice. *Ross. Great.* She decided not to answer him, and instead continued to gaze at the list posted on the wall of the stable at Fair Hill. It was finally March, and time for her first serious competition of the year. Christina and her father had vanned Jazz over to Maryland two days before to give the black mare time to settle into her new surroundings.

Christina saw that she was number fifty-four, and that she was due to ride sixth in dressage.

"How was rehab last year?" Ross asked tauntingly, not put off by her lack of response. "Think you'll go again this summer?" Far from sympathetic, Ross had instead seemed to relish the setback caused by her injury. He had looked positively offended by her insistence on competing last year. This year would be no different.

Christina turned to give Ross a cool look. At sixteen, he was tall and slender, with a horseman's athletic, wiry build. Christina knew a lot of female riders who thought he was adorable. Personally, she found him about as attractive as a garden slug. "I don't think so, Ross," she said evenly. "I'll probably be too busy winning all the meets you're competing in."

Ross's brown eyes narrowed, but Christina turned on her heel and strode smartly away before he could respond. By concentrating, she managed not to have even a trace of a limp as she headed back to Jazz's stall.

The Fair Hill meet took place over two days, with dressage the first day and cross-country and show-jumping the second day. In the morning Christina gave Jazz a light work, then busily groomed her with Kevin's help. Her knee was already aching a bit, but she took some ibuprofen tablets and put it out of her mind. Finally it was her turn to compete, and she rode into the dressage ring.

"Christina Reese, riding Jazz Goddess," the announcer said.

Christina trotted Jazz to the center of the large outdoor ring and touched her fingers to her riding hat in salute to the judges. She began the dressage routine with a thirty-foot circle at an extended trot. In her lessons with Tor, Christina had learned some of the more advanced dressage movements, but they were seldom required for this level of competition. Although she loved the dancelike motions of passage or a pirouette, about the fanciest thing riders at this level ever needed to do was a serpentine at an extended canter. Mostly what the judges were looking for was suppleness, obedience, balance, and grace in the horse.

Christina finished her program with a half-pass toward the judges. Then she drew Jazz to a halt, touched the brim of her hat in salute, and headed out of the ring to where Tor and her father were waiting for her.

"Excellent ride, Chris," Tor said with a smile as she carefully dismounted. "You had perfect form—both of you."

Christina beamed at him. "Thanks. Jazz felt really great, really on her toes. You think we did well?"

"Let's see." Tor listened for the judge's announcement of Christina's score. A huge smile split her face as she heard that she had done very well. In fact, she had only one more fault than Mr. Stinker Townsend himself.

The rest of Fair Hill went very smoothly after that. Cross-country, the next morning, was Jazz's greatest strength, and she showed it, jumping large barriers as if they were only cavalletti. During the midday break Christina ate her lunch in the cab of the pickup truck, her leg stretched out in front of her, her knee wrapped in ice. Her father frowned as he saw her take two ibuprofen tablets.

"It's just for the competition, Dad," Christina reassured him.

"I don't like the idea of you relying on painkillers," he told her bluntly. "It makes me question why you even push yourself like this."

Christina frowned. In truth, she hated taking even the mild over-the-counter medicine also. But she had accepted it as something she had to do to achieve her goal—just as she accepted the fact that after a trial like this she would probably be back in her knee brace for a day or two. "I would probably have to take them even if I wasn't competing," she said in a low voice, but she knew that argument didn't help her case much. Fortunately, her dad decided not to push it just then.

Ross Townsend rode fourth in the show-jumping trial, right before Christina. To Christina's disappointment, he rode perfectly cleanly. Justice, his mount, was eight years old now and in perfect form. Personally, Christina had no respect for Ross's training methods. More than once she had seen him manhandle the horse or take out his frustration on him. He never seemed to blame himself when they performed less than perfectly—it was always Justice's fault. Still, Christina had to admit, the huge chestnut served Ross well, and they were a hard team to beat.

Christina ignored Ross's smirking face as he rode out of the ring. He was greeted by his parents and his little sister, all of whom looked pleased and proud. Brad Townsend had one arm around his wife as he reached up to congratulate his son, and Lavinia was beaming.

In another minute it would be her turn, and Christina double-checked her seat, straightening her back and aligning her legs around Jazz's sleek sides.

"Good luck, Chris," a friendly voice said to her. It was Mandy Jarvis. She walked over to Christina and Jazz. Mandy had been an absolute godsend in the first dark months after Christina's accident. As a child Mandy had been in a car accident and had sustained injuries similar to Christina's. She had been an invaluable source of support and encouragement, and they had remained friends. Christina knew Mandy was trying out for the U.S. Olympic Equestrian Team this summer. She had really come a long way.

"Thanks. You ought to come by the farm soon," Christina said with a smile. "You haven't seen this spring's crop of foals."

Mandy's brown eyes shone. "You know I'm a sucker for baby horses," she said. "I'll be there."

Christina laughed. Then it was her turn to go into the show-jumping ring. After saluting the judges, she turned Jazz and they cantered toward the first jump, a spread fence. Christina felt herself go into her almost trancelike state of concentration as they cleared that jump and turned tightly to the left to take the second. As she had discussed with Tor, she allowed Jazz to take a tiny extra half-stride in the turn, and then they were positioned perfectly for the single wall ahead of them. It was quite high, but with a powerful bound Jazz launched them over it and landed cleanly on the other side. After the wall they tackled six more jumps of varying difficulty, and then suddenly it was over, and Christina turned Jazz to canter out the gap. The sound of applause reached Christina's ears, and she tried to catch her father's eye.

All in all, she thought as she rode out of the ring, they had done well. She knew they had gone clean and thought their time had been right on the mark as well.

At the end of the day the judges read the final scores. Ross Townsend was in first place. Christina was in second with one penalty more than him. A girl named Melissa Sanderson was in third. Christina smiled and thanked the judges when they gave her the second-place ribbon, but it took real effort. If she'd had one fewer fault in dressage, she and Ross would have been tied. Two fewer faults, and she would have won. Since her father had curtailed the number of shows she could enter, she needed to do as well as possible in order to rack up the points necessary for the Rolex Kentucky. She couldn't afford to come in second again.

Her dad and Tor looked as happy and excited about her second-place win as the Townsends looked about Ross's first, but inside, Christina felt far from pleased. Still, she tried to show good sportsmanship and didn't react to Ross's snide smile as he rode past her to lead the winners in a victory gallop.

Later that night, her head resting on her father's shoulder in the pickup, they headed back to Lexington. Tor sat on the other side, enthusiastically discussing the course.

"You know, at Blucher Farms they're going to have another hogback jump, like the one here today," he was saying. "So we'll set up one of those over at Whitebrook. I sure was proud of you today—you're one of the best riders I've ever taught."

Christina smiled sleepily at him. "Thanks. Do you think I'm as good as Mandy Jarvis?"

Tor thought for a moment. "Well, she's older, of course, and has more experience. But you're certainly as good as she was at your age."

A tiny frown creased Christina's brows. "I wish I was better, right now. Do you think it would help if I spent some extra hours on dressage every week?"

Tor laughed. "Yeah, if you want to give up sleeping. Chris, don't worry. You're a fabulous rider, really talented. You can go to the top if you want. Don't be in such a hurry."

"I just want to be the best," Christina said softly.

*　　*　　*

The next afternoon Christina had Jazz in cross-ties in the middle of the aisle and was grooming her after their workout. It was already dark out, and the day had been another chilly, rainy, not-quite-spring day. Leaning her head against Jazz's gleaming black flank, Christina sighed. Jazz reached her head around and whoofed into Christina's hair.

Christina looked up with a smile. Jazz could always improve her mood, no matter how bleak things got. Two and a half years ago, when Christina had still been on crutches, she had often made her way across the stable yard to the training barn. Here, she would sit inside Jazz's stall for hours, sometimes talking to the mare, sometimes silent, sometimes crying as though her heart had been broken. But always, looking into Jazz's intelligent brown eyes, Christina had somehow felt better.

Now she reached up and rubbed Jazz right behind her one white ear, which was cocked and alert. Jazz made a low sound of contentment, almost like a purr.

"Thought I'd find you here." Kevin set down his heavy bucket of feed and came over to Christina. Since the dance, they'd had hardly any time to see each other, except when they were both in the barn doing their chores at the same time. In truth, Christina had felt shy and worried if she'd have anything to say to him now that they'd been on a date.

"Hey," Christina said, trying to sound friendly and normal.

"Have you heard of that movie called *Mile of Glory*?" he asked.

"Sure. It's about Thoroughbred racing. They filmed some of it around here." Christina began working on Jazz's coat with a polishing cloth.

"Well, it just opened at the Galleria, in Lexington. I was wondering if you'd like to go, maybe on Friday night or something."

Christina blushed. Another actual date. She looked up at Kevin and saw the warmth in his green eyes. His dark-red hair was standing up practically on end because he'd been mucking out stalls. Like her, he was wearing ancient, faded jeans, a flannel shirt, and boots so old and dirty their original color was completely obscured. He looked great.

"Yes, I'd like to," she heard herself saying.

"Good." Kevin briefly touched her cheek, then picked up his feed bucket again. "We'll settle the details later."

"Okay, see you." Christina hardly had time to marvel over her new and different relationship with Kevin before her father came out of his office. He looked tired, and he pushed his glasses up on his forehead and rubbed his eyes. Christina knew that he'd been working extra hard lately—

Whitebrook had nearly a dozen horses racing this year, and the season was about to get started. Plus ten new foals had been born in the last two months, and one more was expected any moment.

"You about done here?" he asked.

Christina nodded. "Uh-huh." She unclipped Jazz, then led the filly to her stall. To her surprise, her dad called over one of the grooms and asked him to feed the mare.

"I usually do that," Christina said.

"I know, but I want to talk to you." Her father led the way back to his office, then closed the door behind them. Christina felt a flutter of trepidation. What was this about? Her father looked so serious.

"Let me just jump right in," Mr. Reese said baldly. "I'm concerned about your attitude toward competition."

Christina sat on the beaten-up leather couch, stunned.

"Last year you overcompeted and got yourself into real trouble. You almost had to have another muscle-graft operation. And look at Fair Hill. You were taking painkillers at least once a day and sitting around with ice on your knee whenever you weren't riding. But that's not all. I know quite a few young riders who would have been walking on air after getting second place in a show like Fair Hill. But it wasn't enough for you. You're too hard on yourself, and you're jealous of anyone who does better. Frankly, Christina, I don't like it. I'm getting the feeling that you've changed from being someone who loves horses and loves what she's doing to someone who's competing for the sake of competing and determined to be the best no matter what the personal cost."

He paused for a moment, but Christina still couldn't say anything. She bit her lower lip to keep it from trembling and stared at the cement floor. Her father had never spoken to her this way before, and it hurt. What was worse, she suspected he was right.

"I just lost so much time after the accident," she began feebly.

"Christina, you're only sixteen years old. As a three-day eventer you could compete literally for another thirty years or more. But at the rate you're going, you'll burn out or damage yourself so badly that you'll be washed up by the time you're twenty."

Her eyes wide, Christina stifled a gasp.

"And another point," her dad went on, oblivious to the fact that tears were now rolling slowly down Christina's cheeks. "This whole thing with Ross Townsend. I know he's an irritating snob who thinks he's better than anyone else, but you have to get over it, be bigger than him. I went through the same thing with your mother and Brad and Lavinia, but she eventually learned to ignore them. I want you to forget about competing with Ross. The only person you have to prove anything to is yourself—and I think you already have, haven't you?"

"Oh, Dad," Christina cried, putting her face in her hands and starting to sob. "It's just so important to me! I can't bear losing—especially to him." She felt her father come sit beside her and take her in his arms as though she were a little girl.

"Then you're in the wrong business, sweetie," he murmured. "You're a great rider, but you can't win every single time, and you can't rush your progress. You'll end up losing everything in the end if you do."

"But I just keep thinking about Mom, and how much she did," Christina said through her tears. "She was so much better than me! She almost never lost! Don't you want me to be as good as she was?"

"Oh, Chris," her father said, holding her close. "What I want is for you to be happy and healthy. You're not in competition with your mother—or with anyone. You've helped Jazz become the best horse she can be. You didn't try to turn her into another Wonder, right? The same thing applies to you. All you have to do is be the best Christina you can be—not the best jumper, not the most like your mother. But the best *Christina*. Anything else is just unimportant. Do you understand?"

For long minutes Christina wept in his arms, feeling confusion, anger, and embarrassment. She had been working toward her goal for so long that she didn't know what she'd do if she didn't have it to think about, to structure her life around. Who would she be if she wasn't Christina Reese, her mother's daughter, top jumper on the three-day circuit, headed for the Olympics? Her father held her, stroking her hair, rocking her slightly.

"Shh, honey, shh. Look, I'm not forbidding you to compete. I just want you to think long and hard about what you're doing and why you're doing it. Okay? You know, your mom could be pretty single-minded, too. There were lots of times when she plowed ahead, sure of what she was doing, and all the rest of us just stood around shaking our heads. But she never lost sight of what was important."

Christina's sobs soon quieted to an occasional hiccup.

"I really feel that whatever she did, she was always doing it for the good of the horse," her father continued. "Not for glory, or money, or to show someone up. You can't lose sight of what's important either, honey. You just can't."

Silently Christina nodded, then managed a small, watery smile at her dad. She knew he loved her very much and knew she reminded him constantly of her mother. It would be letting him down to be less of a horsewoman than Ashleigh—to show less fairness, less generosity of spirit. "I'll try, Dad," she said, sniffling. "I promise."

15

THE COOL, DRY MARCH TURNED SLOWLY INTO APRIL. The days grew gradually warmer, the sun stayed a bit longer in the sky. Spring bulbs bloomed in the beds Ashleigh and Samantha had planted so many years before. The new foals went out to pasture with their dams, and Christina, Rebecca, and Kevin spent hours watching them and laughing at their antics. Seeing the small, stilt-legged colts and fillies run after their mothers, chasing each other, nibbling grass for the first time, brought a resurgence of hope and happiness to Christina. This was what it was about: beautiful, healthy, happy horses with the potential, maybe, to someday be champions.

The spring racing season was in full swing, and Mike Reese and Ian McLean had their hands full. With nearly a dozen horses racing, it was the largest

Whitebrook string in years. Two of the three-year-old colts, Blue Dandy and Whitebrook Leader, were showing a lot of promise. Because Christina's show schedule often overlapped with the height of the flat-racing season, she missed several of her father's races, and he missed several of her meets. But she was at Keeneland in early April when Blue Dandy won his first graded-stakes race, beating a Townsend colt, Townsend Warrior.

"A great way to start the year," Samantha said happily as Christina helped her down the grandstand steps at Keeneland. With only a few weeks to go until her baby was due, Samantha was quite big and moved awkwardly. Christina thought she had never been more beautiful.

"Yep—it was a good race, and Blue Dandy ran his heart out. It's exciting to have a colt with so much promise," Christina agreed. True Gift, who had been a champion racer until just the year before, was now at stud at Whitebrook. His first offspring, two colts, were among the latest additions to the farm. Because of True Gift's successes, Whitebrook was now considered one of the finest smaller operations in all of Kentucky.

"You're showing at Blucher Farms next week, aren't you?" Samantha asked as they headed to the winner's circle to congratulate Christina's father and Ian McLean.

"Yep. Think you'll make it?"

Samantha groaned and patted her bulging stomach. "I'll try, but don't hold your breath," she said.

As it turned out, Christina didn't compete at Blucher Farms after all. Three days before the trial, she was working Jazz early in the morning, as usual, when the mare suddenly came up lame. An examination by the vet showed Jazz had a mildly pulled tendon—nothing serious, but she couldn't compete for a week or two. Christina tried to take it in stride. If this had happened a couple of months before, she knew she would have been hysterical with disappointment. But after her father's stern talk, she had tried to put things back into perspective. With the canceling of the Blucher Farms trial, Christina knew it was unlikely that she would get enough points to qualify for the Rolex Kentucky, now only about five weeks away. But she was trying to be philosophical about it—there were several shows later in the summer that were almost as big, almost as important. Her first concern was Jazz.

The next weekend Christina asked Samantha to come over one evening to help her choose new curtains for the farmhouse living room.

"The ones we have now are about thirty years old—they're falling apart," Christina said. "I have a curtain catalog at home, but I need your advice."

"I'll have Tor drive me over around seven thirty," Samantha promised.

Of course, at seven thirty all of Samantha's friends and family were crowded into Christina's kitchen, hiding behind the door and waiting for Samantha and Tor to arrive for their surprise baby shower. Christina and her father had invited practically everyone they knew—all the McLeans; Samantha's best friend, Yvonne Ortez, now Yvonne Curtis; Maureen O'Brien, another of Samantha's friends from high school; Mandy Jarvis and her boyfriend; Grandma and Grandpa Griffen; Caroline and Justin . . .

"I hope I got enough drinks," her dad whispered to Christina.

"I hope I made enough cookies and finger sandwiches," Christina whispered back.

Then the doorbell rang and Christina shushed everyone.

"Now remember, don't come out until you hear their voices," she reminded the excited crowd on her way to open the front door.

"Okay, where's this curtain catalog?" Samantha asked cheerfully, coming inside and taking off her light sweater. "Tor, get ready to take measurements."

"Surprise!" everyone screamed, leaping out from the kitchen. Samantha was so shocked that she almost fell backward into a chair. Tor hadn't suspected a thing either.

For the next two hours Samantha and Tor ate, drank, and opened presents.

"This is great! We won't have to buy a thing!" Samantha declared, her eyes shining with happiness. "You guys are the best friends in the whole world."

The last present Samantha opened came with a card signed, "Love, Jazz." Samantha tore open the wrapping to reveal a small silver picture frame embossed with horse heads in each corner. She gave Christina a fond look. "I'll be sure to thank Jazz before I leave."

"She had a lot of trouble picking it out," Christina admitted.

When Samantha and Tor were ready to go, Christina walked them outside. "So, you got out of Blucher Farms this weekend, but do you think you'll make it to the Greenhall show with me *next* weekend?" she asked. "It's right outside of town."

Ruefully, Samantha shook her head. "I don't think so. The way I feel now, I think the baby's going to come any minute. But if Tor can make it, he definitely will."

"Give me a call if you need anything," Christina said, kissing Samantha on the cheek.

"I will, I promise."

Kevin walked up with the last gift to put in the truck. "See you later, sis. Make sure Tor drives carefully."

"I will." Samantha kissed her brother on the cheek. "I'll talk to you soon."

*　　*　　*

216

But Samantha didn't go into labor that week. Christina saw her or talked to her every day, and knew Sammy was getting impatient as well as weary of carrying all the extra weight.

On Saturday morning, Christina was up extra early to compete in the dressage portion of the Greenhall trial, which was held at a private farm right outside of Lexington. It was a relatively small meet, but considered prestigious. If Christina didn't get a blue ribbon this weekend, then she didn't have a chance of qualifying for the Rolex Kentucky. Rebecca Morrison's parents were going to drive Christina and Rebecca, since Christina's dad was away at a New York track and Tor didn't want to leave Samantha, even just for the day.

Christina was putting Jazz's traveling wraps on when the stable phone rang. She glanced at her watch—barely five o'clock in the morning.

"Hello?"

"Chris, it's Tor. Listen, Sammy's been in labor since midnight, and I'm taking her to Lexington Hospital. She wanted you to know."

"Oh, my gosh!" Christina gasped. "Is she okay?"

"Yeah." Tor sounded tired and tense. "She's fine. I'm a basket case. You have Greenhall today, right? Dressage?"

"Yeah." Christina hesitated. "Do you—does Samantha want me to be there with her? I could maybe . . ."

"Christina Reese!" Tor said. "Don't even think about it. Call the hospital tonight, after you finish. And remember to keep your heels down and your hands loose today, tailbone into the saddle."

Christina laughed. "Okay. Give Sammy my love. And good luck. I'll be thinking about you guys."

"You just think about getting a blue, okay? Bye."

Minutes later the Morrisons came and Christina excitedly gave Rebecca the news while she was loading Jazz into the two-horse van next to Marbella. Rebecca was almost as excited as Christina was.

"I can't wait to find out if it's a boy or a girl!" she exclaimed. "I can't believe Sammy didn't want to know ahead of time."

Soon they arrived at Greenhall Farm, and Christina began to concentrate on the performance ahead. She tried to put all other thoughts out of her mind, but it wasn't easy. Mechanically she settled Jazz in her temporary stall, then went to find her number and her listing. This was the first trial that neither her father, nor Samantha, nor Tor would be watching. Christina felt a nervous flutter in her stomach.

The rest of the day went by in a flash. Once Jazz was prepped and ready and Christina was in her riding habit, all her old instincts took over. She watched the other dressage performances carefully and reminded herself of what problem areas she had to watch out for.

Ross Townsend was riding after her, and he and Justice were already in the saddling ring. A groom was quickly putting extra hoof oil on Justice's hooves so the big horse would look his best. But strangely, Ross's presence didn't affect Christina at all. For the first time ever, she didn't feel the instantaneous rush of anger and tension that he usually caused. It was as though he were a stranger. She could feel his glare boring into her back, but for some reason it just didn't bother her.

Her turn came, and Christina rode into the ring. *This one's for you, Sammy,* she thought. *I'll be with you soon.*

With all the after-show work involved, Christina didn't actually arrive at the hospital until almost six o'clock that evening. Beth and Kevin McLean were waiting for her in the area outside the maternity ward. They were beaming.

"What's the news?" Christina cried, tossing her hard hat onto a plastic seat. She had come right from the meet and was still wearing her riding habit.

"I'm an uncle," Kevin crowed. "I have a niece!"

"It was a girl? Sammy had a girl?" Christina was bouncing up and down, holding on to Beth McLean, whose face was wreathed in smiles.

"She had a perfectly normal delivery, and the baby was born at about one twenty-five this afternoon,"

219

Beth said proudly. "Ian is already on his way back from New York, and your dad will be here by Monday morning."

"Oh, my gosh, I just can't believe it!" Christina cried happily. Kevin gave her a friendly hug, then they all sat down and chatted excitedly about plans for the baby. Soon Tor came out to the waiting area, a huge smile lighting his face. He looked tired, but ecstatic.

"Okay, whose turn is it to visit the little mother?" he asked.

Beth and Kevin both looked at Christina. "We've already been," Beth said. "So you go, Chris."

Inside Samantha's room, Christina tiptoed over to her bed.

"Silly, come over here," Samantha said, grinning. Like Tor, she looked sleepy but thrilled. In her arms was a tiny bundle wrapped in a pink blanket. Awestruck, Christina peered down at the sleeping baby, who just then opened her mouth in a huge yawn.

"It's a filly," Samantha said, her eyes crinkling with laughter.

"Sam! It's a baby, not a horse. You remember that," Tor said sternly.

Christina sat in the easy chair, and Tor put the small bundle into her arms. Her throat choked up as she gazed down at the perfect baby.

"Chris, Tor and I have something we want to talk

to you about," Samantha said, suddenly looking serious. "We were thinking of baby names, and somehow, the only name we really like is Ashleigh. But we wanted to check with you and your dad first."

Ashleigh. After Christina's mother, and Samantha's best friend. "It's perfect," Christina said, her face glowing. "Just perfect. And I know Dad will think so too."

"Really? Oh, thank you, Chris," Samantha said softly. "Which leads us to the second question: Tor and I would be thrilled if you would be one of Ashleigh's godparents. We also want to ask your dad."

For a moment Christina was speechless. A godparent to little Ashleigh! "Try to stop me!" she cried.

Samantha and Tor laughed. "It's all settled, then. Now, you better go home and get some rest. You have a blue ribbon to win tomorrow."

"And in first place, Christina Reese, riding Jazz Goddess. In second place is Hallie Berger, riding Grand Duchess. In third place, Ross Townsend, on Townsend Justice. And in fourth place . . ."

Proudly Christina watched as the judge clipped the Greenhall Farm blue ribbon to Jazz's halter. She wished her father or Tor could be here to see her lead the victory gallop, but she would tell them about it later. As she and Jazz galloped around the edge of the huge outdoor ring, she thought about what this win meant. There were four more shows before the Rolex Kentucky. If she won a blue ribbon at *all* of them, she would qualify to enter.

She was going up against people who had never been injured, had never taken eighteen months out of their training. Her competitors were older and had also entered many more shows over the spring. They'd had more chances to build up their points, both for them and their mounts. She understood what her dad had said about competing, but Christina knew that if she qualified, she would ride in the Rolex Kentucky. And she was going to do her best—her absolute best—to qualify.

16

AS THE WET APRIL SHOWERS GAVE WAY TO THE WARMER, sunnier month of May, the grass-covered paddocks around Whitebrook were a deep emerald green, all the trees were covered with thick leaves, and the early-spring bulbs were replaced by wildflowers and rose blooms.

During April, Christina had earned three more blue ribbons, and she collected the all-important fourth on the first weekend of May. Four days after that, she received her Rolex Kentucky qualification notice in the mail.

"Whew! I guess I don't have to run down to the mailbox every day anymore," she breathed, reading and rereading her letter of acceptance in the farmhouse kitchen.

"Congratulations, honey. I'm proud of you," her father said, leaning down to give her a kiss. "You worked really hard this spring—you and Jazz both. I know I lectured you about being too single-minded, but it's good to see hard work rewarded. You deserve to compete in this trial." He grinned. "And to think, you did it without riding in at least twenty shows."

"I don't know if that made it harder or easier," Christina admitted. "These last four shows, when I knew I had to win, were pretty nerve-wracking. But I remembered what we talked about," she said quickly, looking into her father's blue eyes. "I knew if I didn't get it, I would just try again next year."

"Uh-huh," her dad said dryly. "I guess you're going to give Jazz a few days' rest before next weekend, huh?"

"Yeah. And myself, too. Which is good, because I have to get caught up on my schoolwork." With a final smile, Christina turned and headed up to her bedroom. Once she was inside her room with the door closed, she sank down on her bed. Then, grimacing, she pulled out the bowl of ice that she had hidden under her bed earlier. With quick motions born of three years of experience, she quickly dumped the ice into a towel and wound it tightly around her knee. Then she lay back on her bed and picked up a horse magazine.

Settled against her pillows, she let out a shuddering sigh. The last four weeks, when she had competed in a trial every weekend, had really taken their toll on her. If she had been able to rest in between them, it would have been easier, but of course she still had school every day and was also continuing to work Jazz lightly during the week to keep her in top condition.

"After the Rolex, I'll take it easy for the rest of the summer," she promised herself softly. "Maybe one meet a month. There's a couple of important ones, but I guess I'll skip the National Horse Show this year."

Christina sighed. The ice was helping a bit. She sat up and took two pain tablets. For the past ten days, her knee had been constantly swollen. To compete, she wrapped it tightly in Ace bandages, but she had been terrified her father would notice and yank her out of the competition circuit. However, luck had been with her, and he hadn't actually been able to come to any shows for the past month. Blue Dandy was continuing to be promising, although he had lost the Bluegrass race just three weeks before. But he'd kept Mr. Reese busy.

Christina carefully unwrapped the ice towel for a few minutes. Her knee was still swollen. She fervently hoped she hadn't permanently damaged whatever muscles she had left, but she also knew that nothing was going to stop her now. Even if she was in terrible pain, she knew she was going to compete in the Rolex. Grimly she traced the long pink scars that bisected her knee vertically. This one was from when they put in the artificial joint. This one was from the first muscle graft. This one was from repairing the muscle after she had slipped on some ice and fallen almost two years ago. "I'll probably never wear shorts or a bathing suit again," she muttered. She put the ice back on and lay back down.

Mom, am I being stupid? Would you have done the same? Am I risking too much? Sighing, Christina looked out her bedroom window at the afternoon sun outside.

A few mornings later as she groomed Jazz, she talked over her doubts with the mare.

"Oh, Jazz—what do you think?" Christina asked in a soft voice. "Do you want this as much as I do? Am I pushing you too hard?" She stood back and tried to look at the mare objectively. To her eyes, Jazz had never looked better. She was a supremely toned and muscled animal, with a thick, shiny coat, alert ears, and bright, intelligent eyes. Gently Jazz leaned her head down and whoofed into Christina's long blond hair.

"If I felt that I was hurting you—asking too much . . ."

Jazz stamped her right front hoof.

Putting her arms around the mare's neck, Christina took the weight off her left leg. Her knee was still killing her; it felt as though it were on fire.

There were two days left until the Rolex. She had to make it.

"How are the stars of Whitebrook?" Kevin's gentle voice asked from Jazz's stall door.

Christina turned around with a grin. "I think we've been replaced as stars by Blue Dandy."

"You should have seen him at the Bluegrass," Kevin admitted, his green eyes shining. "Even though he didn't win, he put in an incredible race."

"Later this summer I'll go to more races," Christina promised.

"You two ready for the Rolex? I'm planning to go along as groom."

"Oh, Kevin, thank you. I know I'll feel better if you're there." As soon as the words were out of her mouth, Christina blushed. Although they had been moving slowly and gradually toward being more than just friends, Christina hadn't shown so much of her feelings before.

Kevin smiled, then unhooked the stall door to come stand beside her. "I wouldn't miss it. How's your knee?"

After quickly glancing to make sure no one could overhear, Christina whispered, "It's pretty bad. After the Rolex I'm going to go to bed for a week, I swear."

Chuckling, Kevin said, "Oh, yeah. Sure. I can just see that."

"Well, for a couple days, anyway."

"After you win the Rolex, can I take you out for a celebration dinner? After your week of rest, of course."

Christina's eyes sparkled. "Yeah, I'd like that. Thanks."

"It's a date."

The first day of the Rolex Kentucky dawned cool and misty, with light rain. Since it took place right in Lexington, they hadn't needed to van Jazz over to any temporary stall. At five o'clock in the morning Christina was grooming Jazz in crossties outside her stall at Whitebrook. The mare seemed high-spirited and impatient, as though she knew it was a special day. Christina soothed her as Jazz whoofed out her breath and danced her hindquarters around.

"Okay, girl, okay. Let's just get you prettied up a bit . . ." Christina carefully combed out Jazz's thick, silky mane and set to work braiding it for competition. Kevin was already finishing up Jazz's tail, and now he expertly tied the braid ribbon in a neat bow.

Christina smiled at Jazz, and the mare met her eyes. At times like these, Christina forgot Jazz was a horse: she seemed just like another friend, a person, a sister. The intelligence in those large, long-lashed eyes, the easy communication between them . . . they were connected somehow.

Half an hour later they were loading Jazz into

the Whitebrook van, and then they were off to the fairgrounds, the McLeans' minivan following Christina and her father in the truck.

"We're number sixty-seven," Christina said, tying the number around her waist. Her father helped with the strings. "And we're riding sixth in dressage. Ross is riding second."

"How do you feel?" her dad asked. They had checked in and were due to head to the saddling area in just a few moments. Christina's ears were buzzing. The day before, at her father's insistence, she had been examined by her orthopedic surgeon. He had examined her knee, then frowned down at her over his glasses. Silently, her eyes pleaded with him to give his approval. He had said, "In my opinion, riding isn't doing your knee any good. But if you promise to rest after the Rolex and maybe come in for some more hydrotherapy . . ." Christina had quickly promised. She would have agreed to anything to get out of there. Her father had grudgingly agreed to let her compete, but she had known there wasn't anything in the world that could stop her.

But now she had a knot of tension in her stomach. This was by far the most important trial she'd ever competed in. This morning, while she had been checking in, she had seen two members of the U.S. Equestrian Team checking in also. For a minute, Christina had stood rooted to the ground.

What in the world did she think she was doing, entering a meet against Olympic-class riders? Riders older than she, more experienced; riders without major physical problems that could hold them back. Then she had snapped to, shaken her head, and marched up to the registration desk. She could do it—with Jazz. As a team, they could do it. Christina knew they could. And if they didn't win . . . well, there would be other years.

"Honey, you okay?" her dad asked her, tilting her head up a bit so he could see her eyes.

She nodded. "Yes," she managed to croak.

"I want you to know how proud I am of you," he said seriously. "You and Jazz both. You fought for this horse from the time she was born, and I know she'll do her best by you. And this past spring, watching you compete . . ." Mr. Reese shook his head. "I could see you messing up your knee. I wanted to stop you."

Christina's eyes widened. Her father had known?

"But I decided I couldn't," he continued. "I know your mom would have done the same thing. You *definitely* get your hardheadedness from *her* side of the family." He grinned wryly. "And now you're about to achieve your dream. Good for you, honey."

"Thank you, Dad," Christina whispered, her eyes filling with hot tears.

"Here's something for good luck," Mr. Reese

added, taking a small box out of his pocket. "This was your mother's—now it's yours."

Christina looked at the small velvet box. With trembling hands she opened it, and her mouth fell open when she saw what was inside. It was a charm on a fine gold chain—a charm of a golden Thoroughbred, galloping. There was a framed picture in the living room of her mother wearing this very necklace. "Could you put it on me, please?" Christina asked shakily. Her father fastened it around her neck, and Christina tucked it under her white cravat. The cool gold instantly warmed up against her skin. "Thank you, Dad. Thank you so much—for everything."

Then the advanced-dressage competition was called, and it was time for Christina to head out.

Keep your heels down and your hands relaxed, Christina reminded herself as she trotted Jazz in front of the judges' box. The crowd was completely hushed around them, and Christina tried to forget they were there. Sitting tall in the saddle, she touched her gloved hand to the brim of the formal top hat required for dressage. The judges saluted back.

A light mist was still falling. Christina could feel the tiny raindrops splashing against her face like fine needles as she led Jazz into their first maneuver, a figure eight at a trot. At the top of the eight

231

Christina gave Jazz the signal to change paces, and the mare smoothly switched her leading leg without missing a beat. Christina kept her face impassive, but inwardly she was delighted with how perfectly Jazz was moving. The mare was collected, focused, and patient, responding without hesitation to all of Christina's invisible commands.

They turned again and went into serpentines at an extended trot, then back to figure eights at a canter, and finally into serpentines in the other direction at an extended canter. Christina kept her heels down, her hands relaxed. She was focusing so hard on Jazz and on her own performance that she was completely unaware of her knee.

She and Jazz were moving as one: Christina couldn't tell where she left off and Jazz began. Sitting in the saddle on Jazz's smooth, straight back felt to Christina more natural than walking, more natural than being on the ground. It was what Christina was made for, and Jazz had been made to be her other half.

They finished the dressage program with a half-pass diagonally across the ring toward the judges. With perfect cadence Jazz trotted forward, her body on a diagonal, her forelegs and hindquarters moving on separate "tracks," her shoulders facing forward. It was an unnatural gait demonstrating that Jazz had been well schooled, and that she was obedient and relaxed. And it was perfect.

Jazz came to an instant, smooth stop in front of the judges.

After saluting the judges again, Christina rode into the saddling ring. Her father was there—and so was Samantha, holding a carefully swaddled and rain-proofed baby Ashleigh under her coat.

With a huge smile, Christina dismounted. Her father enveloped her in a bear hug, practically lifting her off the ground.

"Honey, that was beautiful," he said into her ear. "That was riding at its finest."

Christina pulled back and beamed at him. She knew her dad's heart was in flat racing, and sometimes she suspected that he didn't really "get" what she was trying to do with three-day eventing. But now it seemed he did.

"You looked like you were dancing," Samantha said, happy tears in her eyes. "You two were beautiful."

"Thanks," Christina said, feeling shaky. She put her arm around Jazz's neck and began to lead her away. "I have to get her cooled out and dried off before she gets a chill. Come with me, and get my goddaughter out of the rain."

Christina spotted Mandy Jarvis and her horse, a beautiful Holsteiner named Wicked One. She'd known Mandy was competing in the Rolex but hadn't run into her yet.

"Chris! Hi," Mandy called, adjusting her tack.

Christina led Jazz over to her, and the two girls embraced. "I was over at Whitebrook last week—did your dad tell you?" Mandy asked.

Christina grinned and nodded. "Dad says you're looking for a promising retired racer—a horse around seven or eight years old."

"Uh-huh," Mandy confirmed. "You know, I'm using this trial as my leg up into the Olympic team, and I'm going to need to have at least two horses in training. Your dad had a beautiful white mare—I'm thinking about buying her."

"I know the one you mean. She's out of Whitebrook Lass, by Mr. Wonderful. She's great."

"Oh, what am I doing?" Mandy cried. "I'm keeping you here talking in the rain. Go get that mare rubbed down. And I haven't even told you what a fantastic ride you had! What an idiot!" She clapped her hand to her forehead. "But you looked fabulous out there."

Laughing, Christina said, "Thanks. We did our best." With a final wave at the elegant young black woman, Christina led Jazz out of the saddling ring.

On her way back to the Whitebrook horse trailer, she saw Ross Townsend walking around with Justice. He merely dipped his head at her, his eyes cold, and she nodded back at him. She didn't see Brad, his father, anywhere, but his mother was walking with him, an expensive raincoat belted around her waist. She spared Christina a quick, knifelike glance, then looked away. Christina let it roll off her back, just like the rain.

17

CHRISTINA'S SCORE COMING OUT OF DRESSAGE WAS A total of forty-seven faults, which was terrific. Many really good riders averaged about fifty or sixty faults.

The following day was the cross-country part of the Rolex, and Christina arrived early in the morning to walk the course with the other riders. By the top of the second hill, her knee was throbbing and she was trying hard not to limp. She had an hour after lunch before she rode, and she would keep an ice pack on it then, she promised herself.

The course was the longest and most difficult she had ever jumped. Some of the obstacles were almost six feet high, and there were quite a few water jumps and very broad jumps, consisting of multiple poles. By the time she and the other riders had finished walking the course, almost an hour and a half later, she had a knot of apprehension in her gut.

"It's pretty grueling," Mandy murmured as they headed back to the clubhouse.

"It sure is. I haven't had much practice on Irish banks," Christina said. The Irish bank was a hill that Jazz would have to run up, jump an obstacle at the top, then slide down on the other side. It was followed immediately by a huge water jump. Christina bit her lip, understanding that she would have to carry a lot of her own weight as Jazz went over these big, demanding jumps. Her knee was really going to take a beating.

"Last year Michael Young took a spill into a water jump, and Kathy Martins couldn't even finish the course," Mandy said, looking depressed. Michael Young was on the Olympic team and was competing again this year, and Kathy Martins had won the junior hunter championships at the National Horse Show for the last three years. And she hadn't completed the course. Christina swallowed hard.

Three hours later Christina checked Jazz's tack one last time. "You look beautiful, Jazz Goddess," she said softly to the mare. "You're the best, most beautiful horse in the world, aren't you, girl? And we're going to show them all today, aren't we?"

Jazz bobbed her head up and down, as though in agreement, and her ears, one white, one black, flicked forward with eager anticipation.

Christina laughed and kissed the mare's velvety nose. "I love you, girl—no matter what happens. Just help me out today, all right?" Jazz whoofed sweetly against Christina's hard hat.

Ross Townsend had already started the course but hadn't finished yet. Like her, he was too young actually to qualify for the Olympic team, but like her, he was putting himself on the right track. Years from now, they would probably still be competing against each other, Christina thought.

"Need a boost?" Kevin's calm voice inquired. He set a small stool next to Jazz.

"Yeah." Christina grinned self-consciously at him, then her dad came up to kiss her good luck.

"We'll all be in the stands at the finish, rooting for you," he promised.

"Thanks, Dad," Christina said, leaning over to kiss him.

Then it was time for her to head to the course. Kevin gave her hand one last squeeze, and she trotted Jazz off.

At the gate she collected her reins, made sure her helmet was on securely, and pushed her heels well down in the stirrups. A course official gave her the signal to start, and with her heart in her throat, Christina heeled Jazz into a powerful gallop.

They galloped about an eighth of a mile over a sloping hill leading to the first jump, a triple bar about five feet tall and almost as wide. "One, two, three, UP!" Christina cried into Jazz's ear. The tall black Thoroughbred gleefully bounded over the jump and landed lightly on the other side.

The wind was in Christina's face, and though the day was dry, it wasn't sunny. Beneath Jazz's churning hooves Christina could feel wet and muddy divots of grass being thrown up to touch her boots and cling to Jazz's sleek sides. But Jazz gave no sign of being bothered by it. She was racing ahead, eagerly anticipating the next obstacle, as though her favorite thing in the world to do was jump.

A rush of adrenaline and exhilaration raced through Christina's veins. *I love this,* she thought in a split second. *I love this more than anything.* Moving as one, horse and rider flew down wooded paths, leaped over huge post-and-rail jumps, tore across wide meadows, and met every obstacle head-on. As they bounded over treacherous coffin jumps, coops, and blessedly familiar oxers, Christina was only dimly aware of a burning, aching pain radiating from her left knee right up through her hip. By the time they thundered toward the Irish bank, her left leg was almost numb from the relentless, searing pain.

"We can do it, girl!" Christina cried, determined not to let her fearless mare sense her pain and vulnerability. "Here we go, and it's UP!"

Jazz Goddess, her sleek black coat damp with

sweat and gleaming dully in the hazy sunlight, ran without hesitation up the steep forward bank of the jump. At the top she was surprised by the sudden gate jump but took it head-on, bounding over it with a single, powerful thrust. Christina's teeth rattled as they landed, and a low moan was forced from her throat as the landing jarred her knee. But she bit it back and pressed her legs against Jazz's sides as hard as she could. There was no way she would take a spill on this course. No way.

The bank ended abruptly, and Jazz pulled back momentarily as she got into position to slide down the steep bank on the other side. The sharply angled grassy slope had already been turned into a smooth, muddy trail, but Jazz braced her front legs and instinctively used her hind legs to control their descent. Christina loosened the reins as much as she could and leaned way back in the saddle, so that she was almost parallel with Jazz's rump. After a dizzying, slippery rush downward, Jazz reached the bottom and immediately broke into a well-paced canter. Christina straightened up, gulped in a breath, and prepared herself for the water jump, which they were flying toward incredibly fast. With a huge leap Jazz bounded over it, her delicate ankles not even coming close to touching the water. Then Christina hunched over Jazz's withers and yelled, "One more jump, girl—just one more!"

Then they were racing toward the finish line,

where a crowd of spectators lined the fences on both sides. The last jump, a very tall wall painted to look like stones, lay just before them. From where Christina sat, white faced with pain, panting with exertion, it looked insurmountable. But they were barreling toward it, and mechanically she counted strides.

At exactly the right instant, she squeezed with her legs to give Jazz the signal and almost cried out with the burst of pain that followed. Then they were sailing over the jump as though Jazz had wings, and they floated to the ground. It was over. Christina and Jazz galloped through the gate, and the crowd roared.

Numbly Christina drew Jazz back into a canter, then a trot. The mare looked winded and tired, but she had never let up for one instant out on the course. Her black neck was lathered with sweat. Christina started to cry with both pain and relief and happiness. They were far away from the spectators, though she could see her father and Samantha running toward her across the field.

"Oh, girl," Christina said through her tears, "you really came through for me today. You were brilliant—you gave a hundred percent. You made up for my weakness. Thank you, Jazz, thanks. I love you so much."

Jazz whoofed tiredly and continued to trot in a large circle. Slowly her breathing calmed, and soon they were walking through the thick grass. Still Christina wept silently, the pain in her leg making her whole body feel numb and stiff. For so long she had worked to get this far, and now that they were here, she felt overwhelmed by emotion.

Oh, Mom—it seems worth it to me. Am I okay? Do you think I've done the right thing?

"Honey, are you all right?" Her father took Jazz's bridle, and the mare obediently stopped.

Christina, white faced, practically fell off the saddle into her father's arms. On the ground she leaned against him, her left boot resting lightly on her right foot. Quietly she cried against his shirt and his broad, comforting chest while he unsnapped her hard hat and stroked her hair.

After quickly kissing Christina's cheek, Samantha took Jazz's bridle and began to lead her back to the stabling area. Jazz had to be cleaned up before being vanned home again.

"Wait," Christina said in a broken voice. "I wanted to wash her off. She worked so hard today—"

"Kevin and I will do it," Samantha said firmly, in a voice that didn't allow disagreement. "You go sit in the truck and have a cold drink."

Christina held on to her father's arm as she hobbled painfully to the Whitebrook pickup. Soon she had taken two pain tablets and was drinking an icy soda that tasted like heaven. A heavy towel packed

242

with crushed ice was wrapped around her knee. From where she was sitting, she could see Kevin and Samantha shampooing Jazz, lathering all the dirt and sweat off her thick coat. Jazz was tossing her head and giving the occasional whinny. She loved being bathed.

With a happy sigh, Christina leaned back against the truck seat. She felt a hundred percent better. Then she caught her father's eye. Her father was looking at her with a concerned expression on his face. For a panicked moment Christina feared that her dad would insist she drop out of the competition. She dreaded the argument they would have if he did—she just couldn't back out now.

"You did great today, sweetheart," was all he said, though there were lines of worry around his mouth and eyes. "I'd say you have a shot at a trophy."

"Can you believe how fantastic Jazz was today?" Christina said. "She knew what I wanted her to do even before I knew it."

Her father grinned at her. "I guess you were right about that mare."

"You better believe it!" Christina declared.

After a good night's rest, she and Jazz had both been back to fighting trim for the third day of competition. The mare had eaten a good dinner the night before, and her legs had been sound, not stressed or overworked. Christina had stayed in bed at home all evening, her leg propped up on a pillow, as Rebecca, Kevin, Samantha, Tor, baby Ashleigh, and practically everyone else she knew came to visit.

After the grueling cross-country competition, the show-jumping part of the trail had seemed—well, not easy, exactly, but definitely doable. At the end of it, the inseparable team of Christina and Jazz had been in third place, which was a terrific achievement for their first Rolex.

That afternoon, just as the sun was beginning to sink toward the horizon, Christina stood on a white-painted stand in the middle of the large ring. In the middle, on the highest stand, Mandy Jarvis beamed proudly. On Mandy's other side was Michael Young, who was on the U.S. Olympic team.

"We're very proud and happy to announce that Amanda Jarvis, riding Wicked One, is this year's first-place winner of the Rolex Kentucky!" the judge said into a microphone. The crowd cheered and clapped. Christina, still in her official riding habit from the show-jumping competition, smiled. Then the judge announced Michael's name, and then Christina's, in third place. Glancing out to the stands, she could see her family and friends waving, clapping, and whistling their approval.

Now the judge presented Christina with a small silver trophy, engraved with "Rolex Kentucky" and the year. It felt heavy in her hands, and her eyes were suddenly glazed with tears of joy. She knew she hadn't gotten to this point alone—so many people had helped her along the way, encouraged her, supported her: her father, Samantha, Tor, Kevin, Rebecca . . . and her mother's voice, which had picked her up when she was at her lowest, soothed her when she was full of pain and sorrow, and urged her to continue when she was at the end of her rope. *Thank you, Mom*, she thought now, holding the silver trophy above her head, listening to the cheering of the crowd. *Thanks for being with me—thanks for everything. I love you. I'll always love you.*

EPILOGUE

MIKE HAD GONE HOME ONLY ONCE SINCE CHRISTMAS Eve, briefly, to shower and change, then he was back at Ashleigh's side in her hospital room. For the last twenty-four hours, doctors had been pumping medicine into her.

"It's a good sign that there's been no change," Dr. Maystrom had told him earlier. "Her blood pressure has remained stable, and both her heart and brain functions look great. Let's just wait for her to wake up."

So he had been waiting. He'd also gone to check on baby Christina, who was doing fine—she was off the respirator and bawling loudly.

The door to Ashleigh's room opened, and a white-garbed nurse came in.

"Mr. Reese?" she said softly. "I had an idea . . . it's strictly against the rules, but . . ." She motioned to another nurse standing behind her, who entered the room carrying a swathed bundle. Mike immediately recognized the small pink features of his daughter.

"We thought maybe being around her baby would help," the nurse whispered, placing Christina in Mike's arms. Gratefully he nodded, then stood by Ashleigh's bed, rocking Christina. She was very small and had fine blond down covering her head. The nurses had dressed her in a soft cotton nightgown and put bootees on the tiny feet. Mike smiled tiredly down at her, and the baby yawned and opened her eyes.

Mike propped Christina up in his arms so she could see Ashleigh. "That's your mommy," he said softly. "Isn't she beautiful? She's sleeping right now, but I know she's going to wake up soon, because she wants to see you. She loves you very much." Mike's voice broke and he cleared his throat, then continued rocking Christina. On impulse, he held the baby closer to Ashleigh. Christina was wide awake, with the alert, solemn expression babies often had. Suddenly the little booted feet kicked, and Christina's small fist, no bigger than an apricot, reached out to touch Ashleigh's face. Quickly Mike pulled the baby back, shushing her and rocking her again.

"Mike?" The quiet voice, so beloved, so familiar, was so shocking to hear that Mike almost dropped

Christina. He gasped when he realized Ashleigh's eyes were open, and she was smiling sleepily at him.

"Ash—honey, oh, thank God you're awake!"

"Mmm, I'm fine," Ashleigh said groggily. "Let me see our baby."

Hardly able to breathe or speak, Mike held Christina back down toward her mother. "Oh, Ash, I've been scared to death," he whispered. "I've been so worried about you."

Slowly Ashleigh raised one hand, still with a tube in her arm, and brushed her pale fingertips against Christina's soft, peachlike skin. The baby cooed and wriggled in Mike's arms. He felt like crying. "Christina," Ashleigh breathed. "I've been dreaming about you. I missed you."

Turning loving eyes toward her husband, Ashleigh said, "Did I miss Christmas?"

He nodded. "But we can have our own Christmas, now that you're better."

Ashleigh smiled, then put her finger against the baby's palm. Christina's tiny fist closed around it as though she would never let go.

Two days later, Ashleigh awoke feeling much more like herself. The doctors had determined that she would have no lasting damage from the tiny damaged vessel in her brain. She was ready to get on with her life—her new life as a mother.

Right after breakfast, several nurses crowded

into her room, their faces wreathed in smiles. Ashleigh laughed with delight when they held up Christina, dressed in the smallest Santa Claus outfit Ashleigh had ever seen. "Oh, come here, precious," Ashleigh said, holding out her arms. "Let Mommy see you."

"Your husband is outside," one of the nurses told her, a twinkle in her eye. "If your doctor was here and saw what you were being taken home in, she'd never let you go. But don't worry, we won't tell her."

"What is it? What has he done now?" Ashleigh asked, a smile spreading across her face.

"Well," one of the nurses said evasively. "It snowed hard last night, and it's a real mess outside . . . But Mr. Reese seems awfully determined to take you two home today . . ."

Ashleigh was mystified, but concentrated on dressing herself warmly, then wrapped Christina in a soft blanket so only the tip of her pink nose was showing. The nurses wheeled Ashleigh and Christina to the hospital door, and there Ashleigh got her answer. Outside it was a gray afternoon, and snow was falling. A thick blanket of snow already covered everything. It looked like a fairyland: the trees were draped in white icicles, and the world looked clean and quiet. Then Ashleigh saw her surprise.

"A horse-drawn sleigh!" Ashleigh gasped, her eyes wide.

Sure enough, Mike was waiting outside with a beautiful old-fashioned sleigh. A dark, sturdy horse was harnessed to the front, and it was stamping its feet excitedly in the snow, its breath puffing out in little white clouds.

"Oh, Mike, this is perfect," Ashleigh cried as Mike came to help her out of the wheelchair. "It's just perfect."

"Everyone's waiting for you at home," Mike said. "We haven't even opened presents yet."

"But where did you get the sleigh?" Ashleigh asked, climbing carefully into the front seat. Mike placed Christina in her arms, then draped a warm woolen blanket over both of them, tucking them in firmly.

"Tor had it back in his barn," Mike explained, climbing in himself and picking up the reins. He clicked his tongue and shook the reins, and the horse trotted off gaily, its strong legs punching through the snow. Golden sleigh bells jingled in the crisp, wintry air, and Ashleigh snuggled close to Mike.

"This is the most perfect Christmas ever," she said happily, her eyes shining. "Absolutely the most perfect Christmas ever."

Pulling aside the blanket, she gazed down at her small daughter, Christina, who looked up at her. "I love you, darling," Ashleigh whispered down to the baby. "I love you, and I'll always be there for you—always."